THE MOTIVE

KHURRUM RAHMAN

ONE PLACE. MANY STORIES

HQ
An imprint of HarperCollins*Publishers* Ltd
1 London Bridge Street
London SE1 9GF

www.harpercollins.co.uk

HarperCollins*Publishers*
1st Floor, Watermarque Building, Ringsend Road,
Dublin 4, Ireland

This edition 2021

1
First published in Great Britain by
HQ, an imprint of HarperCollins*Publishers* Ltd 2021

Copyright © Khurrum Rahman 2021

Khurrum Rahman asserts the moral right to be
identified as the author of this work.
A catalogue record for this book is
available from the British Library.

ISBN: 978-0-00-840444-4

MIX
Paper from
responsible sources
FSC
www.fsc.org   FSC™ C007454

This book is produced from independently certified FSC™ paper
to ensure responsible forest management.

For more information visit: www.harpercollins.co.uk/green

This book is set in 12/16 pt. Stone Serif

Printed and bound in Great Britain by
CPI Group (UK) Ltd, Croydon, CR0 4YY

For those who think they can't. I feel you.

THE MOTIVE

Thanks to your help, we're getting the nation reading!

1 in 6 adults in the UK struggles with reading. Buying this Quick Read could change someone's life. For every Quick Read sold, a copy will be donated to someone who finds reading difficult. From mental health to social mobility, reading has a proven positive impact on life's big challenges. Find out more: readingagency.org.uk @readingagency #QuickReads

Born in Karachi, Pakistan in 1975, Khurrum moved to England when he was one. He is a west London boy and now lives in Berkshire with his wife and two sons. Khurrum is currently working as a Senior IT Officer but his real love is writing. His first two books in the Jay Qasim series, *East of Hounslow* and *Homegrown Hero*, have been shortlisted for the Theakstons Old Peculier Crime Novel of the Year and CWA John Creasey Debut Dagger.

Also by Khurrum Rahman

East of Hounslow
Homegrown Hero
Ride or Die

Chapter 1

June 23rd, 2016. Brexit Referendum.

'Do you love me?' Sahira asked.

It was not what Conrad expected. Not there. Not in such a public place.

He smiled. Boyish. Cool. The same smile that he flashed at Sahira on the first day of the first term, in their accounting and finance lecture. The same smile that she fell for and broke tradition for.

'Yeah, course I do,' Conrad replied, as he casually draped an arm over the back of the booth.

Sahira placed her hands on the table and fidgeted with her car keys, which were attached to a heart-shaped key ring.

'Say it,' she said, her brown eyes meeting blue. 'Say the words.'

Conrad's smile froze in place, less cocksure now. 'What's going on, Sahira? Everything okay?'

'Just…' She looked into Conrad's eyes. 'I want you to say it.'

Her demands and her appearance made her look a little crazy. Conrad had never seen Sahira looking anything less than perfect. But now her perfect straight hair was tied painfully tight in a bun, and her perfect face showed every flaw without the usual touch of make-up.

'Here? Now?' Conrad glanced over his shoulder. Creams Dessert Lounge was full of students he'd seen around the campus, students that he'd partied with. Some that he'd been intimate with. All playing a small and fleeting part in his life. 'Place is packed. We ought to be careful. Right?'

They were so different in so many ways. Most of all skin colour. He was white. She was beautifully brown. His family background was money and success and privilege. Sahira's background was a strict Muslim upbringing in a humble immigrant household. This was why for eight months Conrad and Sahira had kept their relationship quiet. Status mattered. Religion mattered more.

To the outside world, they were fellow students. Nothing more. Sahira had told him many times that acting or speaking inappropriately in the wrong place could lead to a vicious rebuke from a ruthless community. A community that Conrad didn't know much about.

'I need to know,' Sahira said. Her gaze and the focus in her voice had him squirming. 'I really need you to tell me, right now.'

Conrad dropped his arm from the booth and placed his hands on the table close to hers. The tips of his fingers flicking the tips of hers. He liked her a lot. But, love? Conrad wasn't sure. He'd never felt like this with anyone before. Maybe in the last eight months they had crossed the line from a casual fling to something more serious.

Maybe it was love.

'I love you,' he said, squeezing it out in a whisper in case of being heard. It wasn't that saying it bothered him. He'd said it to her plenty of times before, but in private.

Everything that defined them as a couple was done in private.

Sahira placed her hands on top of his. An intimate gesture that couldn't be mistaken.

'I love you too,' she said.

Conrad kept his eyes on her, when he really wanted to check if anybody was watching them. They'd always been so careful. Sahira had shown him what was and wasn't OK in a public place. Declaring their love in the middle of Creams Dessert Lounge, with students that they both knew knocking about, was breaking the rules.

Something had changed.

The last thing Conrad needed was change. His life was perfect. He'd smashed through his final exams, and tonight he was holding a house party to celebrate. He'd planned to buy liquor, score some coke, and sort out his party playlist.

This, whatever this was, wasn't part of his plans. Conrad had to squash it quickly.

'You're acting... strange. What going on with you?' he asked, trying to keep his tone neutral, but his heart was thumping as his brain filled with scenes that only she could remove.

Sahira leaned forward over the table and took a small breath.

'We should get married,' she said.

Suddenly, Sahira's hands felt like a heavy weight on his.

A waitress in a bubble-gum pink uniform hovered over them. She eyed them curiously in turn before deciding that it was none of her business. She held up a small pad, a small pencil poised over it.

It gave Conrad an excuse to slip his hands away from Sahira's. He fumbled with the oversized menu and opened it in front of his face, his alarm hidden for a moment.

The waitress kept tapping her pencil on the pad, in time with her foot tapping a beat on the tiles. From the slight safety of his place behind the menu, Conrad's eyes wandered around the dessert lounge. Were people looking at them?

Hannah, a girl he had once dated, and who he still saw when the mood took him, was watching Conrad in open-mouthed awe. She was not going to be happy.

Conrad smiled tightly at Hannah before looking back at the menu. His favourite desserts suddenly all seemed too sweet and sickly. He wondered if they had a drinks menu. He could do with something hard. Then he remembered that he didn't drink. Not in Sahira's presence.

The waitress cleared her throat.

'Sprite, please,' Conrad mumbled. The waitress continued to eye him. 'Just Sprite!' he repeated, sharply.

The waitress rolled her eyes and turned to Sahira, but she shook her head. The waitress walked away muttering to herself.

Conrad put the menu down on the table and hoped his face didn't give away his thoughts.

'Sorry,' he said, not quite sure what he was sorry for. 'What were you saying?'

'You heard,' Sahira replied curtly.

'We're not even engaged.'

'So,' she shrugged, 'we'll get engaged.'

'Baby, baby, baby,' he said, trying to reclaim

some of that cool he was known for. 'What's the rush?'

'I have to show my family that you're not messing me about.'

'Wait!' Conrad panicked. 'Do they know about us?' It was no wonder that Sahira was being so open with him in public. If her family knew about their relationship, then who was there left to hide it from? 'I thought you said–'

'No,' she cut him off, 'they don't know. But it's only a matter of time. We need to get married. This summer. Before we leave college.'

'What the fuck, Sahira!?' Conrad was immediately aware that he'd said the wrong thing, aware that he had said the wrong thing loudly. The noise around him died down. Eyes searched and found the source of the outburst. 'The hell you all looking at?' he screeched, and the noise slowly started again, but hushed now. His name and business were whispered from mouth to ear. Half of these gossips had been invited to his party. He shook his head clear of it.

Conrad could've – and probably should've – got up and walked away. He didn't owe Sahira a damn thing. It wouldn't be the first time he'd done that when a relationship had become too intense.

12

Marriage?! *Christ.* They were both only twenty years old.

It wasn't too late. Whatever she was going through, Conrad would help her see sense. He looked across the table at Sahira. Her gaze hadn't left him. She looked absolutely certain.

Conrad had to play the game that he had mastered.

'Look, Sahira…' His face formed a pained expression. 'Me and you, we've got it good. I love being with you, being around you,' he said, and it brought a small smile to her face. It was a good sign. He went on. 'But marriage? I mean, why now? We're both so young–'

Sahira opened her mouth to speak.

'Please, listen to me a minute. Let's get this summer out of the way. Once we've left uni, you and I, we'll find work, make some money, *save* some money, just like we talked about. Then, yeah, in a year or two's time… We'll get married.'

'Conrad–'

'I mean, that's the easy part,' he laughed. 'The hard bit will be finding a way of breaking it to your family. But… but we'll figure it out, yeah, you and me, we'll figure it out.'

Conrad sat back in his chair, running it over in his head. Did she believe him? She wouldn't be the first. However, Sahira wasn't like the other

13

girls. He couldn't just drop her in an instant, not in the state that she was in. The knock-on effects would be a mess. What if she told an older brother, or someone from the scary Muslim community? Conrad had heard stories about how over-protective they could be about their girls. Truth be told, it's part of what attracted him to Sahira in the first place.

The challenge. Touching the untouchable.

No, he couldn't just walk away yet. He would have to find a way to ease himself out of this relationship.

Conrad smiled to himself. Sahira smiled at him. Whatever foolish notion had been swimming in her head seemed to have drowned.

'What do you think?' Conrad asked.

'You paint quite the picture,' Sahira replied, warmer now, seemingly back to her usual self. 'With you by my side, we can get through anything. I think you're going to make a great dad.'

His smile froze in place. His mind struggled to work out what she meant. Did she mean *one day* he'd make a great dad, like years and years down the line, or did she mean something else?

Conrad swallowed. He had to know, he had to hear the words.

'What… what are you saying?'

Sahira's smile blossomed. She reached out and took his hands, which were slick with sweat. She locked her fingers between his, and said, 'I'm pregnant.'

Chapter 2

Jay

I pulled up at the polling station, and left my Nova in the small school car park. I picked up the polling card and looked at it. The name stated Javid Qasim. Even though that's what my parents called me, it looked strange. I never thought that name suited me. If I were you, I wouldn't bother wrapping my lips around it. Keep it simple.

Call me Jay.

I stepped out of my car and walked across the car park towards the polling station. I sighed to myself. Dickheads! I swear, dickheads were out in force. Asians on one side, a mix of the youth and the elderly. On the other side, white folk, the same mix. Battle lines well and truly drawn. Only thing that separated these clowns was the pebbly path that led to the polling station. Both sides remained calm, but beneath it I could feel the nervous energy bubbling as they looked for the smallest of excuses to kick off.

16

I walked the path between them, clutching my polling card with my head down. I didn't want any part of this shit, but I could sense judgement, as they easily worked out which way I'd vote just from the colour of my skin.

They'd be right.

I was given the ballot paper on entering the polling station. In the wobbly booth I checked the options.

Remain a member of the European Union.
Leave the European Union.

In. Out.

In. Out.

Shake it all about.

I put a tick against *Remain* and then noticed that it should have been a cross. With a swoop of the tiny pencil I turned the tick into a cross. It now resembled a swastika. *Fuck's sake!* I folded the paper in half and dropped it in the ballot box.

I walked out the way I came in, with muted cheers from one side and whispered sneers from the other. A hero to some, a villain to others.

Fucking jokers, the lot of 'em.

I wasn't like them. Looking for a fight that they could never win. As a young British Paki, I had to keep my head down. I didn't need friction at my door.

17

What's the point?

I walked away from them and jumped into my clapped-out red Vauxhall Nova and checked my phone. No messages, no missed calls. Business was slow and I had a rucksack full of Hounslow's finest weed in the boot of my car to shift. I sighed heavily. I didn't really want to go back to an empty house. Mum was on a date – she didn't actually say she was on a date, but the shimmering dress she was rocking told me that she was out to impress. I shrugged to myself. At least one of us was enjoying ourselves.

I checked the time. It was almost hitting nine. I could still save the night. I thought of calling Idris, my closest friend. But I knew he'd be as busy as a crime-fighting bee. I couldn't keep up with his shift patterns ever since he'd become a cop. I tried my luck.

'OK, Google,' I said in the direction of my phone. 'Call Idris.'

My phone just stared blankly back at me. Google wasn't in the mood. It never was. I don't know why I bothered. I picked up my phone and did that shit the old-school way.

'Yes, yes, Idris,' I said. 'What you sayin'?'

'What you sayin', Jay?' came back his deeper voice.

'I just cast my vote. Not that there's any point.

18

It's not like we're willingly going to leave Europe,' I said. 'You voted?'

'Nah,' he said, and before he could make excuses, I was on him.

'You gotta vote! There's still time. Go!'

'Didn't you just say there's no point?'

'I did say that,' I said. 'But still, stranger things have happened.'

'I can't, anyway,' he said. 'I'm working.'

'Just as well,' I said. 'Knowing you, you probably would've voted *Leave* anyway.'

'Fuck off.' He laughed, but I think it struck a chord. Idris was as brown as they come, but he sometimes veered to the light side. I think the scientific term is 'coconut'.

'So, what? You chasing bad guys round the block?'

'I'm on a stake-out with my partner. Can't say too much about it, but I think something big is about to go down.'

'Cool,' I said, feeling a little sorry for myself. The night ahead of me wasn't even close to being as exciting as my friend's. 'When you knocking off?' I asked. 'Wanna shoot some pool?'

'No can do. I'm on the late shift,' Idris said. 'Tomorrow?'

'Yeah, tomorrow,' I said, and checked out.

I looked across the car park towards the polling

station. The two sides were still making eyes at each other. I shook my head and put the key in the ignition. With fingers crossed I turned the key. The engine coughed into life and I drove out of the car park.

I was around ten G short of upgrading the Nova to a black 5 series Beemer. To achieve that I was going to have to sell a lot of weed, but lately it'd been slow. I rattled my Nova through Hounslow, slowing at all the familiar haunts, hoping to clock some familiar faces looking to score. It's always slow in the summer. People preferred to be sitting in a pub getting merry rather than sitting at home getting high.

I was just about to call it a night and head home when my phone rang. It was a number I didn't recognise. I answered it and placed it on speaker. I could hear loud muffled music in the background.

'Who's this?' I said.

'Is that Jay?' a nervous tinny voice came back at me.

'You called me,' I said, suspicious enough not to confirm my name. 'Who're you?'

'Duncan,' he said. 'I got your number from Chinese Ali. He said you could, uh, sort me out.'

'Did he now?' I replied. 'Well, Chinese Ali's getting a slap, next time I see him.'

Honestly, Chinese Ali was getting no more than a polite word. His nickname came from his taste for martial arts.

'So… Can you arrange something, please?' Duncan pleaded.

Every instinct told me to end the call. With each one of my customers, I made it my business to know their business. I didn't deal to strangers. It was way too risky.

'We've just finished end-of-year exams,' Duncan said, 'and we're having a house party to celebrate.'

Students? House party?

That got my attention.

A house party for a dealer is as good as a winning lottery ticket – and that 5 series wasn't going to land on my lap.

I swear, being broke makes a person reach stupid decisions.

'All right,' I sighed. 'Where you at?'

Chapter 3

Idris

We'd left the patrol car in the lay-by, climbed the wooden gates and stomped five minutes on uneven ground through straw fields, until we were hidden behind a large oak tree.

Just so we could have a cigarette.

It had to be that way. A copper in uniform couldn't be seen smoking in view of the public.

'Tell me you got a light,' I asked my partner, Police Constable Jennifer Stepson.

Stepson frowned as she patted one pocket and then the other. I looked longingly towards the patrol car that we had left in the lay-by. The lighter was probably sitting in the centre console.

'Got it,' Stepson said, slipping it out from the inside of her stab vest.

She sparked me up first and then herself, and tucked the lighter back inside her vest.

I leaned back against the tree. She stood in

front of me as we both disappeared briefly under a cloud of smoke.

Stepson was about fifteen years older than me, I guess. Obviously, I wouldn't dare ask. Even though we were the same rank, she acted like my senior, because she once *was* my senior. Stepson had been demoted to police constable for taking a hard line against a couple of youths that she'd pulled over.

The youths were Asian and, of course, they'd said she was racist and their complaint went to the top of the Hounslow Met. It made the local press, and she was confined to desk duties before they let her back on the field, in a much lesser role.

Unlike PC Stepson I was heading in the opposite direction, itching to step up into the role of detective inspector.

I was more than ready.

'Who was that on the phone?' Stepson asked.

'Just a mate,' I replied, knowing what was coming next.

'Why'd you tell him you were on a stake-out?'

'I don't know,' I replied, 'keeping up appearances, I guess.'

'Why? Is your mate like a high flyer or something, so you got to impress him?'

Jay? A high flyer?

23

I laughed. 'He ain't even been on an aeroplane.'

'So what then? Don't tell me you're embarrassed, Zaidi?'

'What've we done today?' I asked. 'Read the riot act to a teenage girl who'd pocketed a sandwich from the local Sainsbury's, and held up a speed gun to clock anyone doing over thirty miles per hour. Seriously, I don't think I can take much more excitement.'

'They've got you on the fast-track programme. You'll make DI within a year. In the meantime, stop feeling sorry for yourself. You're doing my head in.'

Stepson was right. I'd applied successfully for the fast-track programme. My law degree helped and, if I'm honest, probably the colour of my skin, too. It didn't bother me – I was on my way to becoming a DI. But it did bug me that some of the older detectives looked down at those who are fast-tracked. And some of the older, *whiter* detectives looked down at those who progress just so a fucking box could be ticked. It made me want to try harder. Prove to them old codgers that I'm more than just a token Paki in a uniform.

The only way I could change their view of me was to prove my worth. But there wasn't much chance of doing that, plodding the streets of Hounslow as a constable.

The police radio attached to Stepson's vest crackled to life. I rolled my eyes wondering what our next exciting adventure would be – moving along a homeless guy, or cautioning a pissed couple for shagging behind the bins in a pub car park? I rubbed my face and then moved away from the tree so I could finish my smoke in peace before having to face the humdrum orders. I smoked it down to the butt and pinched it out between my fingers. I didn't dare throw it down on the field. Stepson had given me one too many bollockings for littering.

I walked back towards her as she finished the call, and I could tell immediately that she was in shock.

Something had gone down.

I walked faster just as my heart beat faster, and met her by the oak tree.

'What?' I said, wide eyed. 'What is it?'

Stepson looked up at me, her mouth open in surprise, as though she couldn't comprehend the nature of the call.

'Stepson,' I said. 'What the fuck?'

'We have to go right now,' she said.

'Where?' I said.

'A house party on Lampton Road.'

'Shit! What went down?' I said, trying to keep the excitement out of my voice.

Jenny locked into my eyes. 'The neighbours…
They've complained about the noise.'

'Oh, very fucking funny!'

I stomped away across the field back to the
patrol car, with Stepson's laughter echoing in
my ears.

Chapter 4

Jay

I didn't need to check the door number that Duncan had texted me. I could hear the music blaring from inside the house as I cruised past searching for a parking spot.

There's a risk of the unknown, dealing at somebody's house. You never know if someone's going to turn on you, and it's why I tend to deal straight out of my car. I should've belled Duncan back and told him to pop outside, so I could give him his gear and bounce. But I swear, this party looked like it was off the hook, and each one of those students was a likely customer.

I stepped out of the car and took my rucksack, full of the finest A-grade skunk, from the boot. I slipped both my arms through the straps and walked with my eyes peeled – either for cops looking to collar me, or for some rival dealer looking to jump me and steal my stash.

I looked up at the double-fronted house as

I walked down the wide path. This pad wasn't your usual student digs. Whoever was living here had Mummy and Daddy eating out of the palm of their hand.

I got to the front door and jabbed at the door bell, knowing full well that I wouldn't be heard over the music. I put some pressure on the front door. It clicked open. I pushed it all the way and the wall of noise and music swept through me.

I stepped into the house, bopping my head to the tune and adding a little bounce to my walk, so as not to stand out. The music wasn't to my taste, but it was loud and I was feeling it. In the hallway there were a few nerdy-looking guys hanging with each other, not yet brave or drunk enough to enter the main part of the house among the beautiful people.

The song faded out and before the next one kicked in, I approached the nerds. They were all wispy hair and novelty T-shirts of bands that were around way before their time.

'Yo,' I said to them. 'Any of you know where Duncan is?'

They shook their heads at me blankly. The music kicked in again. A sik beat with shit lyrics – like all music nowadays, all style and no substance. I sent out a text to Duncan to let him know I was in the house.

Behind me the front door opened and closed.

A middle-aged Asian man entered looking more out of place than I did. He looked pretty fucked off, truth be told. He wore a snarl on his face, and judging by his thick build, I had no doubt it could be backed up with a bite. I assumed he was a neighbour who had an early shift the next morning at the airport, and was pissed off at the loud music keeping him from the beauty sleep that he sorely needed.

The nerds seemed to sense danger as only nerds can, and made themselves small against the wall, as the man eyed each of us in turn before dismissing us. Thankfully we weren't the target of his anger. I'd hate to be the person who was.

The man stomped past us, rudely barging against my shoulder as though I wasn't there.

I made my feelings very fucking clear, under my breath, and he went into a room to the left. I figured I didn't have much time before he shut the party down.

I turned and faced the nerd patrol.

'You boys know where I can get some weed from?' I asked.

'No,' one said, the light reflecting off the metal braces wrapped around his teeth.

'We wouldn't mind some ourselves,' another sighed, looking pained.

'Is that right?' I smiled.

*

They bought small and I didn't accept any money from them. Instead, as payment, I asked them to spread the word. And spread it they fucking did. By the time I helped myself to a vodka and lemonade from the makeshift bar, I was king.

I set up at the kitchen island, perched upon a high stool, as students started to orbit around me for their ganja fix.

Thirty minutes in, my rucksack felt lighter, and I had a whole new clientele, who had now rushed into the garden to smoke the finest skunk this side of Amsterdam. I'd lost count of how much money I'd made.

I felt movement behind me, and turned to see somebody looking full-on dismal.

'Help you, mate?' I asked.

'I've been searching for you?' he said, a hint of posh that sticks out in a place like Hounslow.

'Duncan?'

'Yes,' he said.

I nodded. He looked like a Duncan, awkwardly tall with bad posture.

'I texted you, was waiting for you to reply,' I said, glancing at my phone. 'Oh shit. You did reply. Sorry, I got a little busy.' I unzipped my rucksack. 'How much you after?'

Duncan fiddled with his phone and I could see the note he'd made on it. 'Can I, um, get an eight ball please?'

'Nah, man, I don't deal that shit. You want coke, you're gonna have to whistle for it.'

'But Chinese Ali said–'

'Don't care what Chinese Ali said. I don't deal cocaine. You want some skunk or not?' I asked, starting to get cross. I hated muddles.

Duncan looked nervously over his shoulder. The party was flowing, a mix of alcohol and weed and shit music. The room was alive around us.

'I don't know, let me find out,' Duncan said, and made a phone call. No one answered. I shook my head at him so he knew I wasn't happy. 'Sorry,' he said, looking pretty sorry. 'I can't get through to Conrad.'

Conrad! What the fuck? I bet my life that he's the only Conrad knocking about Hounslow.

'The music's too loud. He probably can't hear the phone,' Duncan said. 'Let me go up and ask him. Do you mind waiting here a minute? I'll be quick.'

I felt sorry for him. He was just a gopher

trying to score for a friend. I didn't really want him tramping up and down the stairs passing messages between us. I might as well deal directly with whoever the fuck this Conrad was.

'Take me to him,' I said.

I followed him through the crowd, out of the kitchen and up the stairs.

'I've never seen a student yard like this before,' I said, over his shoulder. 'Let's hope the landlord doesn't find out about this little shindig.'

He stopped halfway up the stairs and turned to answer. 'It's not like that. It's Conrad's place. Well, not *his* exactly, but his father's.'

I smiled. Something about him made me. The way he stopped to answer. I nodded my head for him to keep moving.

'Oh, right.'

'So where you from?' I said, checking out his blue chinos and shirt combo. He definitely wasn't local.

'Marlow,' he said, without stopping to answer this time. 'We didn't quite make the grades to attend the uni of our choice, so we… you know.'

'You ended up in Hounslow,' I said, as we hit the landing. 'I didn't think there was a uni around here. Not much demand for it.'

'University of West London,' Duncan replied. 'Down the road from here in Brentford.'

I made a mental note. Another customer base where I could ply my trade, thank you very much!

I stood behind him on the landing as he knocked on a bedroom door.

'Hannah!' he spoke through the door. 'It's me.'

A fumble with the lock and Hannah opened the door, a pretty blonde who looked as if she knew it. She glanced past Duncan and eyed me curiously. 'Conrad told you to keep everyone downstairs.'

'Yes, I know. This is the, uh, dealer. He hasn't got any coke? Only weed.'

'God!' Hannah said, looking back over her shoulder at a boy sitting on the edge of the bed. He had his head in his hands. 'He really could do with a line about now.'

'Can't help you,' I said, and made to leave.

'No, don't go. Come in, let me speak with Conrad,' she said.

Duncan stepped into the room. I shrugged and followed. Hannah shut the door behind us, drowning the music out.

'Conrad, hey baby,' she said, in a very different voice, sweet and sickly. 'We can't get any coke?'

Conrad groaned behind his hands, before removing them from his face. I took him in, a crisp white shirt tucked into ironed dark blue denim jeans, turned up at the bottom. On his feet were maroon suede loafers. And no sign of socks.

It made me feel awkward.

He swept a hand through his floppy blond hair, and asked me, 'Speed?'

'No, man. No speed, no coke and no pills. I don't do any of that shit. You want some weed then I'm your man, otherwise I'm gonna bounce.' I checked my watch as though I had somewhere to be. I didn't.

Conrad looked across at Duncan and nodded.

They hadn't told me how much they wanted, or asked what it cost. It was clear they weren't blazers. These were rich kids with a liking for rich kids' drugs. I could have taken them for a ride, but fuck man, even I have some sort of moral standards.

I took a small Ziploc bag from my rucksack. 'It's quite compact but that's a decent size teenth,' I said, handing it to Duncan. 'That's gonna be a score.'

Duncan looked across at Hannah, clearly confused. She shrugged blankly at him. He looked back at me. 'Sorry, a what?'

'Twenty quid, mate,' I sighed.

Duncan placed a crisp twenty in my hand, and I handed him the weed.

'You got skins?' I asked. 'Rizla?'

Duncan shook his head.

'You ever blaze before?' I asked, slipping out my own packet of king-size silver Rizla.

'I... No,' Duncan replied. 'I've never taken any drugs. It's just...' He discreetly gestured over his shoulder towards Conrad and whispered, 'He's going through some problems right now. He just needs something to take the edge off it.'

I looked over. Hannah was knelt down in front of Conrad, making wide eyes at him as she rubbed his arm. 'I'm here for you,' she said softly. 'Whatever you need.'

Not my business.

I pocketed the twenty quid. Duncan stared at the bag of weed in one hand and the skins in the other as though trying to figure out the key to the fucking universe.

'Do you want me to wrap one for you?' I asked.

Chapter 5

Idris

'To be fair,' Stepson said, 'it is pretty loud.'

'Yeah,' I muttered, 'crime of the century.' I held down the bell and waited a few seconds before hammering against the door with the side of my fist. I waited, wishing I could be anywhere but there. Impatience quickly turned to frustration when nobody answered.

Stepson dropped the handle and pushed. The door opened. She smiled proudly.

'Let's get this over and done with,' I said. 'After you.'

Before we could step inside, a voice from behind us said, 'I'm so sorry.'

We turned to face a woman. She was too old to be a student, but not old enough to be old. Attractive, in a modest way. She wore a knee-length skirt and had her arms folded over a navy-blue cardigan.

'I'll get them to turn the music down,' she

said, and stepped past us and stood at the door. Her small frame didn't fill the doorway, but was enough to tell us that we were no longer necessary.

'And you are?' Stepson eyed her curiously.

'Sarah. Sarah Braithwaite. I'm a lecturer at the college.' She smiled. 'Most of these are my students, and they're celebrating the end of their exams.'

We stood in the porch a little awkwardly. Stepson nodded her head for longer than necessary, as if she was thinking things over.

'I'll get them to turn the music down,' Ms Braithwaite repeated. 'I'd rather this not get back to the head of faculty. He's a lot less forgiving than me. So… if you'll both excuse me.' She smiled nervously before politely shutting the door in our faces.

Sarah Braithwaite had made it clear that she'd deal with it, and, honestly, it was a waste of police time. We could have been better placed at polling stations, where shit was bound to kick off between the Remainers and the Brexiteers.

'I guess we're not needed here,' I said, more than happy to leave.

We walked out of the house and headed for the patrol car.

'I didn't like her, little Sarah Braithwaite,' Stepson said, for no apparent reason. She was like that, quick to make a snap judgement. Copper's instinct and all that. She walked around to the driver's side and I stood by the passenger side door. The music was still blaring from the house.

I eyed Stepson over the roof of the car. Something was bugging me.

'What is it?' she asked.

I scrunched my face, trying to figure if I should say what was running through my mind. 'Nothing, it's just…'

'Spit it out, Zaidi.'

'Way I see it,' I said, 'we've just walked away from a house full of drunk, rowdy students, and we're sending a lone female teacher in to shut down their party.'

I knew Stepson well enough to know that she would pick up on my blatant sexism. She lifted an eyebrow long enough to make a point.

'Attractive,' she said with a mock smile. 'You didn't mention attractive.'

'I don't know what you're talking about.' I mock-smiled her right back.

'So you're thinking that we should head back in and rescue the damsel?'

'I don't really want to be here. I'm just saying

I'm not sure how it's going to play out; a teacher rocking up at a house party. It could get messy. And listen…' I nodded my head back towards the house. 'Music's still blaring. They're probably ignoring her as we speak. We may have to pull rank.'

Stepson thought about it for all of a heartbeat.

*

We entered the house. We're not monsters. We weren't there to shut it down and take the fun away from the little fuckers. We'd ask the host politely to turn the music down and then we could be on our way. If, and I mean *if*, we happened to bump into Sarah Braithwaite again, then we'd put it down to chance. And if I played my cards right I could even leave with her number.

At the end of the hallway, Stepson and I split up. We'd know as soon as the other had any success when the damn racket died down. She stepped into the kitchen to the right and I moved into the living room.

Immediately the partygoers buttoned up as soon as they saw me, and my uniform. Chinese whispers bounced from ear to ear. The mixture of anxiety and excitement was plain. I was used to such a reaction, so I ignored it and took in my surroundings.

I'd been to a few house parties back when I was at uni, normally in run-down terraced houses, where everyone was cramped in and sweaty, and an amateur DJ broke into each song with the next, blaring it through distorted speakers. Nothing like this, never in a place that looked like this.

This was all high ceilings and whitewashed walls, and instead of the retro posters that students seemed to love, there was art on canvas. I couldn't tell if it was expensive, but it didn't look cheap. There was a white sideboard running across the length of the far wall, posh-looking finger food was laid out neatly in trays, with bread rolls and cut meats and cheeses that I didn't recognise. Back in my day, we'd have settled for a bowl of crisps. Bottles of liquor were lined up beside the food, and there were glass tumblers instead of plastic cups.

The biggest thing I'd noticed was that the music was crisp and coming from wireless speakers fitted into the ceiling throughout the house. It made life a little difficult. If there'd been a DJ, I could have clipped him around the ear and told him to ease up on the volume.

Instead I'd have to go hunting for the host of the party.

I made eye contact with a grungy sort, the type that lives on a skateboard. I leaned in so he could hear me over the music. The smell of weed came off him in waves. 'Whose party is this?'

'I, um... huh?' he said.

I snapped my fingers in his face. He flinched and his eyes widened before his pupils centred.

'Conrad,' he said. 'Don't know his surname. I don't even know him that well.' He swallowed. 'Can I... Can I go now please?'

'On your way,' I gestured with my head before he started to cry.

'No one's seen him all night,' a voice said from behind me. I turned to see a group of girls sipping colourful drinks that matched their colourful outfits.

'Any idea where I can find him?' I asked.

'You're not the only one looking for him,' one said, which made the others giggle.

'What does he look like?' I asked, growing annoyed.

'Sooo good-looking!' another purred, and it set them off again.

'Right. Great. Thanks,' I said, as I wondered how they would get on under questioning.

'Oh, there is one more thing. If you see Sarah Braithwaite, let her know I'm looking for her?'

That knocked the smile off their faces.

The one thing worse than a copper turning up at a house party is a teacher.

Or a parent.

Chapter 6

Jay

I was sitting on a high-backed chair, which was working wonders for my lumbar region, hunched over a pine desk. I think it was pine. I'm not up on wood, but it didn't look like it came from Ikea. On the desk was a lamp, neatly stacked textbooks, and an open MacBook Pro laptop. This was steadily going through a music playlist which was being beamed through the ceiling speakers downstairs. I was tempted to play something to my taste, but didn't think gangsta rap was suitable for that generation's sensitive ears. Above the desk was a large mirror. It seemed like young Conrad liked to watch himself while he studied. Yeah, it figures.

Duncan was peering over my shoulder, watching me at work as I put the finishing touches to the joint. He seemed fascinated. He should be. It's a fine art. I gently tapped the end of the joint on the flat surface of the desk to level the mix of skunk and tobacco. Then I held it under the table lamp and inspected it. It was tight, with not a crease in sight. I looked over my shoulder and Duncan gave me a serious nod of approval.

I handed it to him and he took it with great care into the palm of both hands, but it was quickly ripped away from him by Hannah, without any care for the build.

I shook my head. Duncan, fast learner that he is, copied my gesture. The joint had now made its way to Conrad and was resting between his dry lips. Hannah got a lighter and sparked him. He coughed and spluttered on the first pull like a fucking amateur, before settling into it.

'More,' Conrad said. 'Get him to roll some more.'

Him!

'Jay,' I said with a little attitude. 'And roll it your fucking self. I'm out.'

Duncan looked at me, pleading.

'For fuck's sake,' I said under my breath, and went way beyond my call of duty and started to build another joint.

I was starting to notice the dynamics of this little group, and I didn't like it. Conrad seemed like a twat and a bit of a bully whilst Hannah fawned all over him in the hope that he would notice her. It was clear Duncan wanted to be there as much as I did, which was not very much.

Through the mirror, I watched Conrad take a pull, and disappear behind a cloud of smoke. Hannah was beside him on the bed. 'That's it, relax,' she cooed, resting her head on his shoulder.

'I… I can't,' Conrad said.

'Tell me what happened,' Hannah asked. 'How did she take it?'

'I don't know. As soon as she said the words, I walked away.' Conrad dropped his head in his hands. 'I fucked up.'

'You've done nothing wrong, baby.'

'She's been calling and texting me all day. I've just… I've just ignored her.'

'It's probably for the best,' Hannah said, and then smiled. 'We'll get through this.'

'We?' Conrad snorted.

'I've told you, I'm here for you,' Hannah replied. 'Whatever you need.'

'Yeah? Are you going to help raise the baby?'

Talk about being a fly on the fucking wall! I was trying not to listen, but I couldn't help but steal glances at them through the mirror. I could feel Duncan cringeing over my shoulder.

'You don't have to do anything you don't

want to,' Hannah went on. 'I'm going to sound like a bitch here but, honestly, it's her problem. Besides... she has options.'

'Abortion,' Conrad nodded blankly.

It went silent for a minute. The spliff changed hands from Conrad to Hannah. I lined up the Rizla with some weed, and tried to block out the noise as I focused on the muffled bass running through the house.

'I could talk to her,' Hannah said, as though she'd been running through the scene in her head. 'I'll show her that she's ruining her life, I'll even offer to go with her to the clinic.'

'I don't think so,' Conrad said. 'She can't stand you.'

Hannah seemed taken aback by that. 'Fucking Sahira Hussain!' she hissed. 'She's going to ruin everything.'

I froze. It lasted a millisecond. But I definitely froze. I don't know anyone by the name of Sahira Hussain. But the thought of this selfish fuck making a Muslim girl pregnant, and then discussing how to weasel out of his duties made my blood boil.

I had to correct myself. I had to fucking tell myself that this had nothing to do with me.

Why should it make a difference that it was Muslim girl?

I finished rolling the joint in hurry. I didn't bother checking it, but I knew it was loose and creased as fuck. I handed it over my shoulder to Duncan and stood up. I didn't need to be there a second longer. I grabbed my rucksack, and slung it on my back, my arms through both straps. Every bit of skunk I had was gone and replaced with cold hard cash. I'd done good business, but I knew I'd be leaving the house feeling like shit.

'I'm done here,' I said, leaving no room for argument.

Duncan wasn't about to give me one. 'Thanks,' he said, looking almost as uncomfortable as me.

'Yeah,' I said, dropping my eyes in fear of giving away my emotions. I didn't even bother to speak to Conrad and Hannah. I knew that if I did, I'd be doing a lot more than fucking speaking to them.

I opened the bedroom door and stepped out onto the landing. The music hit me hard and washed over me. As I walked down the stairs I slipped out my phone. There were no messages. No offers or invites. I could've stayed, had a drink or two and mingled with the dudes and the nerds and the hot uni girls, but I wasn't in the mood. It was time to call it a night and go home.

I slipped my phone back into my pocket and noticed the same Asian man that I'd clocked when I arrived. He was walking heavily up the stairs towards me. What I hadn't noticed earlier was that his eyes were veined red, and he had a look on his face that I wouldn't want to fuck with. He looked like a man who had been pushed too far, and who was certain that he was going to shut this party down.

I moved to one side, giving him room to walk past me on the stairs. He slipped past me as though I wasn't there.

I got to the bottom and felt the mood of the house party had changed. There was some tension that hadn't been there before. I poked my head into the living room. Nobody was dancing, or drinking, or having any fun. It was as though someone had pressed pause. I figured the cause of it was the female copper strutting around like she owned the place.

A part of me wondered if, maybe, she was a stripper, but her clunky shoes told me otherwise. That, and the fact that she was making everyone fucking nervous.

Including me.

I may not have been carrying skunk any more, but I was carrying a rucksack which very much smelt like skunk and was loaded with bills. If

I was searched, I'd have to answer some tricky questions. I backed quietly out of the living room and into the hallway, ready to make a hasty exit. But just my fucking luck, I backed into another copper.

Chapter 7

Idris

His rucksack pushed against my midriff and he spun around quickly. His face formed a picture of horror when he noticed the police uniform. That horror turned quickly to relief, followed by an all too familiar goofy smile when he looked up at my face.

'Oh, man,' Jay grinned. 'Idris! The fuck you doing here?'

We bumped fists. 'What's happening, Jay?' I said, not able to hide my smile at seeing my best friend.

'Thought you were on a stake-out?' he said, knowingly. '"Something big is about to go down." Isn't that what you said?'

'Yeah, you know. That finished earlier than expected, so...'

'So what?' Jay grinned, taking a great deal of pleasure out of it. 'Let me guess, one of the neighbours complained about the noise and you came running?'

'All right, Jay,' I said, 'don't take the piss.'

'No, no, I'm not,' Jay said. 'You're doing a lot more with your life than I am. You don't have to play the big man with me.'

'I know that,' I said, and *I did know that*. Jay was the last person who would judge me. 'Anyway, you want to tell me what *you're* doing here? Bit old to be at a student party, aren't you?'

'You know.' Jay looked away, and shuffled awkwardly. 'Just chillin'.'

My eyes went to his rucksack. 'Jesus, Jay!' I snapped at him before glancing over his shoulder at Stepson, working the living room. I caught her eye. She gave me a nod and I returned it with a tight smile. 'You can't be doing that here!' I hissed at Jay through clenched teeth.

He gave me a shrug that said, *this is exactly where I should be doing it.*

I returned it with a pained shake of the head, as I tried to figure out how to deal with him.

'Don't sweat it, I'm dry,' Jay said. 'It's all gone.'

'All gone, is it?' I said. 'I'm guessing your bag full of weed is now a bag full of cash.'

Jay looked suitably sheepish as he nodded his head. I started to get a little worried for my stupid friend.

I've known Jay all my life, literally! We were born within days of each other, at the same hospital. Our mothers became friends, and that meant that we became friends. And even though we'd taken very different paths – I, an officer of the law and he, a drug dealer – we have always been tight. I didn't blame him for his choice of work. Jay grew up without an old man and, though he'd never admit it, I think he craved the guidance that only a father can give.

Even as an officer of the law, I put our friendship first. I'd always turned a blind eye to his dealings. I mean, it's not like he's Scarface. He's juggling nothing stronger than a little weed on the streets of Hounslow, so I let it be. But I'm pretty sure that any other copper would not be so relaxed about it.

'Idiot!' I said, glancing over his shoulder. Stepson was speaking sternly to a couple of guilty-looking lads. They were pointing directly at Jay. It was clear that they'd just given up the hand that fed them.

'Get rid of the rucksack, right now,' I snapped at Jay. Over his shoulder the crowd seemed to part, allowing Stepson a clear path to us.

'Stepson,' I nodded, as she stepped out of the living room and stood beside me in the hallway. 'Any luck finding the host?'

'No, something else grabbed my attention,' she said, fixing her eyes on Jay.

I tried to keep my eyes off Jay, tried not to notice his Adam's apple bob and weave, as I silently prayed that he wouldn't do anything stupid like make a dash for it. As it stood, Jay had managed to shift all of his stash, so he couldn't really be done for possession with intent to supply. But, if searched, Jay would have a hard time explaining a rucksack full of cash.

'What's your name?' Stepson asked Jay. My heart was beating fast on his behalf.

'Jay,' he shrugged, trying to play it cool. 'You wanna tell me yours?'

She shot him a look before replying. 'PC Stepson.'

Jay leaned his shoulder against the wall and crossed his legs at the ankles. 'Why don't you give me your real name?' He smiled. 'What do your friends call you when you're not in uniform?'

Oh, for the love of God. He was trying to flirt with her. I knew the signs from his many failed attempts. It was awkward for all concerned. Rightly, Stepson ignored his clumsy banter. 'What's in the rucksack?' she asked.

'My jumper. It gets a little chilly at night. A bottle of water. And, uh, some books.'

Shit! He was doing so well until he mentioned books. No one was buying that crap.

'I'm going to ask you to remove your rucksack,'

Stepson said, not giving it up. Jay's eyes shot up at me.

'Stepson, trust me. He isn't worth the paperwork.'

'We get him under the lights he may give up the name of his supplier?'

'Listen to your partner.' Jay smiled. 'I'm really not worth the paperwork.'

Stepson ignored him and leaned in close to me, her blue eyes measuring mine.

'I thought you wanted to be taken seriously, Zaidi.'

'I do. I'm saying he'll get away with nothing more than a caution. I can't be bothered dealing with this nickel-and-dime bullshit. Let's just get the music turned down and go.'

Stepson leaned away, and exhaled loudly as she took a moment to think. I turned to look at Jay. He was still leaning sideways against the wall, a picture of cool. But I knew him well enough to know that he was shitting himself. I gave him the smallest of nods to show that he had nothing to worry about.

I was wrong.

Stepson stepped around me and faced Jay. 'Hand over your rucksack.'

I had been naïve to think that Jay's misguided life choices would not mess with mine. There was nothing I could do for my friend. If Stepson wanted to carry out her job, I didn't have the power to stop her. Jay's face was a picture of the childhood innocence that I once knew, as he looked at his friend to get him out of trouble. All I could do was give him a sad smile.

Defeated, Jay took one arm from the strap and then the other and held it out. Stepson reached over to take it by the strap, but just as her hand was hanging in mid-air, a crashing sound loud enough to be heard over the music stopped her in her tracks. She looked up towards the ceiling. I followed her gaze. The ceiling light was swinging from side to side as though somebody in the room above was breakdancing. Then a silence for a long second made it seem as though we'd misheard. But there was no mistaking the crunching sound of smashed glass that followed.

Stepson's hand dropped away from the rucksack, and she stormed off up the stairs.

'Get the hell out of here!' I hissed at Jay, as I rushed after Stepson, taking two steps at a time. At the top of the stairs, I glanced down. Jay was leaving the house and shutting the door behind him. He had no idea how close he came to being caught.

I stood beside Stepson on the landing, facing

the bedroom door where we'd heard the sound. Stepson pounded on the door with the side of her fist. 'This is the police!' she called, loud and clear. 'Is everything all right in there?'

'*Fuck off!*' a deep voice growled.

And then a weak voice screamed, '*Help!*'

I turned the handle, the door was locked from the inside. Every cop wants to kick down a door. Honestly, it's one of the perks of an otherwise boring job. I glanced at Stepson. She nodded, and moved aside to give me some space. I took one step back, placing my weight on my back leg, and kicked. The sole of my size tens made contact with the sweet spot right under the handle. The door flung open and crashed against the wall.

I froze for a moment at the sight in front of me.

A man with his back to me was straddling a squirming body. He turned at the waist and made eye contact with me. I noticed that he was Asian and old. Way too old to be at a student house party.

He screwed his face up tightly and looked me dead in the eyes. Then with no regard to the police uniform, he turned away and threw a heavy fist into the face of whoever was underneath him.

'Move!' Stepson screamed from behind me. She pushed me into the room and into action.

I moved quickly and wrapped my arm around

the man's throat. Over his shoulder I could see the victim. He was only a young lad. His right eye was shut and swollen to a pulp, and blood was oozing from his forehead. I tightened my grip, my bicep hardening against the man's throat, and leaned back hard, my legs doing most of the work. But the man was strong and fucking determined. He was able to raise his arm and throw a final punch before I managed to pull him away, sprawling onto my back and taking him with me.

I held him firmly in my grip. At the edge of my peripheral vision I noticed, for the first time, a young girl cowering in the corner of the room, her knees tucked under her chin, crying uncontrollably. I caught her eye and nodded that *it's okay, you're okay*.

I took my eyes off her and looked at Stepson. She was standing over us. In her hand she held a canister of CS gas.

'It's cool,' I said, fully out of breath. 'I've secured him.'

Maybe she didn't hear me, or maybe she didn't agree with me, because the next thing I knew, Stepson held up the canister and started to spray.

My head was close to the man's and I was in the line of fire. I squeezed my eyes tightly shut and tilted my head away as Stepson sprayed the fucking gas into the man's eyes. He started to wriggle violently in my grip as the burning sensation set in. Quickly his breath became ragged. I loosened my grip from around his throat.

'That's enough,' I screamed through closed eyes, but I could still hear the hiss of the spray. I was acutely aware that too much tear gas could kill somebody who suffered from asthma or other lung diseases. 'Stepson, it's fucking enough!'

The hissing stopped.

Ignoring the stinging sensation on my skin, I opened my eyes. The boy was sitting up, and watching through one eye. He'd taken a good beating, but he didn't seem in need of urgent medical assistance. But the man in my arms did. He was limp now. His ragged breathing had slowed. Really fucking slowed.

I couldn't have him dying, not on my watch. Not in my arms.

Smoke was hanging heavy in the air from two joints burning freely in an ashtray. It was the last thing the man needed if he was finding it hard to breathe.

I had to get him out of the room.

I shifted out from under him, lifted from under his arms and tried to drag him out of the room so I could examine him. 'I need a fucking hand,' I cried, looking up at Stepson.

Her eyes didn't leave mine as she took her sweet fucking time attaching the CS spray back to her belt.

I knew then, when PC Stepson and I wrote our incident reports, our accounts would be very different.

Chapter 8

Jay

Holy fucking moly, Batman. That was way too close.

That female copper did not like me. But there was something else. I don't know, I couldn't put my finger on it, but she looked at me as though she had already decided that I was guilty.

Which I was! But still, give a brother the benefit of the doubt.

I shrugged to myself, and locked my rucksack in the boot of my Nova. I looked back at the house. Music was still blaring, crisp and loud. And now Idris had turned up, my aim of calling it a night had changed. I couldn't remember the last time me and Idris had kicked it at a house party. Obviously I knew he was there on duty, but, fuck it, beggars can't be choosers. It might still be a laugh.

I headed back to the house, knowing Idris wouldn't be happy to see me at first. But trust me, he'll mellow. Besides, I'd got shot of the rucksack, so he no longer had a conflict of interest.

I searched for Idris in the living room first, and then the kitchen, but couldn't spot him anywhere. The party was full-on again, and I knew that wouldn't be the case if the fuzz was still knocking about. But I knew they had to be there somewhere, because their ugly cop car was still parked outside on a double yellow.

I went upstairs and turned the corner.

Through the open bedroom door, I saw Idris. He was bent over a man, trying desperately to lift him from under his arms.

'Give me a fucking hand,' he screamed at his partner. Without thinking I stepped into the room. Idris' eyes widened when he saw me, but he realised quickly that this wasn't the time to be giving me a bollocking. 'Help me, Jay,' he said.

He didn't have to ask twice. I stepped inside and took hold of the man's legs. I saw instantly that it was the pissed-off Asian guy who I'd seen earlier. Idris gave me the nod and I returned it, and together we lifted him. Fuck, he was heavy, and my legs were trembling, but I managed to help carry the man out of the bedroom.

'See if any of those doors are open,' Idris said.

Still holding onto the man's legs, I used my elbow to drop down the handle of a door and used my shoulder to push it. We hauled the man through into a bedroom and placed him gently on the bed.

I took a moment to catch my breath. Idris didn't have time for that. He rushed across the room and opened the window, and then he was back on the man, checking for a pulse.

I couldn't help. I'm ashamed to admit that I'm pretty useless at first aid, but I was feeling pretty fucking proud of seeing my friend in action.

I bent at the waist and rested my hands against my knees, and looked around the bedroom. It was smaller than Conrad's, and neater. I realised that we were in Duncan's room. Sitting on a tidy desk was a framed photo of him and, I assumed, his parents, judging by the awkward smile they all seemed to share.

'Jay,' Idris snapped. 'Get Stepson in here, now!'

I rushed out of the room and cut across the hallway into Conrad's bedroom where, not twenty minutes ago, I had been rolling a couple of joints.

The fuck had happened in there after I'd left?

Conrad was sitting on the floor slumped against the foot of the bed, looking like he'd just got knocked the fuck out. Hannah was on nurse duty, lovingly consoling him through heavy sobs. Past them I noticed the mirror above the desk was smashed, and the shards of glass left hanging in the frame were smeared in blood.

Seriously! What the fuck happened?!

Did the old man ask Conrad to turn the volume down so he could get a good night's kip? And knowing Conrad, from the five minutes that I spent in his company, did he arrogantly tell him to do one, and the man... what? Threw him head-first into the mirror?

Stepson stepped in front of me.

'Idris wants you,' I said, and instantly cursed silently under my breath. 'I mean, PC Zaidi.'

Too late, her brain was turning behind her eyes. I'd fucked up! Calling him by his first name implied a relationship. A relationship between an officer of the law and a drug dealer.

She spent a moment or two taking my measure, as if there wasn't a fucking bigger picture. 'Don't leave this room,' Stepson said to Conrad and Hannah. 'I'll be back to take your statements.'

Stepson walked out of the room. I was about to turn and follow, but I couldn't take my eyes away from Hannah and Conrad. She was holding him tightly, her face a mess of mascara and tears as she gently ran a hand through his blond hair. Breathlessly, she kept repeating, 'It's just you and me... It's just you and me... It's just you and me.'

Conrad seemingly fuddled, replied in the same breathless tone.

'*Sahira.*'

Hannah's hand stopped running through his hair. Her body seemed to stiffen. No doubt the name she despised ran through her mind. I could no longer watch. I quietly moonwalked out of the room and shut the door on the soap opera.

From one drama to another. I stepped back into Duncan's room. The Asian man was still on the bed, and his eyes were now open, but barely. Stepson eyed Idris like a hawk as he patted the man down, stopping as he felt something in the man's trouser pocket. Idris slipped his hand in the pocket and brought it out clutching an inhaler. He lifted the man up into a sitting position against the headboard. Seeing Idris shaking and rattling the inhaler, the man managed to open his mouth. Idris placed the mouthpiece between his lips. The man inhaled slowly and deeply as Idris pressed down on the inhaler.

'Did you get his name?' Stepson asked, coldly.

Idris shook his head. 'He's only just come round!'

The man looked around the room blankly, and blinked weakly, as though he didn't know where he was or what he'd done.

'What happened to him?' I asked.

Neither Idris nor Stepson answered, but they shared a look which I couldn't work out. Stepson was the first to speak. 'Well, ask him his name!'

'Can you call for a damn ambulance first?' Idris said.

Stepson reached for her radio. 'Then we can ask him what he thought he was doing attacking the boy,' she said.

As soon as the words had left her mouth, the man's eyes widened and his chest rose. In one quick movement he pushed himself off the bed, and reaching to his full height he growled, 'I'll fucking kill him.'

Idris stepped in front of him, hands out in front of the man's chest in a calming manner. The man swatted his arms away, catching Idris by surprise. Before he could react, the man landed a vicious head-butt to his nose.

'Fuck,' Idris dropped to one knee, one hand holding his bloody nose, the other trying desperately to grasp the man.

But he was on the move.

Stepson stood in his path. With a flick of the wrist, she pulled out her baton, but the man was too close for her to take a full swing at him. He grabbed her arm and forced her back like they were in some sort of fucked-up foxtrot, until the back of her head bounced against the wall. He let go of her arms, and Stepson slid down helplessly onto her haunches, wincing and holding her head.

The man turned to face me. I was standing blocking the door. I swallowed. I was so far out of my element. Fuck, man, I'm a lover, not a fighter, and he didn't look like he was in a mood for romance.

'Listen,' I smiled. 'Mate,' I said, but before I could charm him, his shoulder connected plum with my jaw and the room flipped upside down as I landed on my back.

I blinked and squinted at the ceiling light. A second – or two, or three – later, Idris stepped over me and rushed past, followed by Stepson. They crossed the landing, and I turned my head just in time to see them rush into Conrad's bedroom.

'Step away from the bed,' I heard Idris say. He sounded calm despite being attacked, although his voice was a little muffled on account of his nose being busted.

I sat up and shook my head clear. I gradually got to my knees, my neck slightly strained from when I'd landed on my arse. I wondered if I had whiplash. I wondered if I had an injury claim. I lifted myself off my knees and stumbled across to Conrad's bedroom. Feeling a little light-headed, I held onto the doorframe for support.

'Take two steps back and put your hands behind your fucking head,' Stepson screamed. She was the total opposite of Idris. She held up a canister – I assumed some sort of tear gas – in one hand, and the baton in the other. I couldn't see what they were facing, as both Idris and Stepson were blocking my view. I tiptoed and peeked over Idris' shoulder, but quickly dropped back down to the flats of my feet and squeezed my eyes shut.

I'd seen enough.

But that image wouldn't leave me. Conrad curled up on his bed, bleeding over the sheets. A knife dug in his side. The Asian man was standing over him.

When he'd threatened to kill Conrad, not for a second did I think he'd go through with it.

Chapter 9

Idris

Before Stepson was demoted to police constable, I'm certain she'd witnessed events like this. She had experience which I lacked. But I couldn't help but feel that the situation required some talking. It required calm.

'Lower it,' I said to Stepson, through the side of my mouth.

Stepson ignored me. The CS canister remained high in one hand and, in the other, her fingers were tightly wrapped around a baton. The mood she had been in, she wasn't about to back down.

'Step away from the fucking bed!' Stepson screamed at the man.

My hands were held high, too, but in an attempt to calm him. I could see in the man's face that he knew he'd gone too far. His eyes were as wide as his mouth, and he was shaking his head continually as though he was in a state of disbelief.

I looked at the boy. He was curled up and bleeding on the bed. With his eyes closed, he looked younger. Though we were a couple of metres apart, I could still see the knife planted between his ribs moving slightly with every small breath he took.

'He's still alive,' I said.

The man stopped shaking his head, and his wide eyes moved over to the boy.

As it stood, the charges he would face were serious, but they were a lot less serious than murder. He looked away from the boy and up at me. Relief showed in his face. With Stepson beside me just fucking ready to go, I wanted him to keep his eyes on me and me alone.

'We just need to get him some help,' I said softly, maintaining eye contact.

'This is not what I wanted,' the man said.

Stepson snorted. I tried to blank her out. 'Sure,' I continued to address him, 'we can talk about that?' I was blagging my way through this. I didn't have the training for such an event, but I had to find a way through to him and I sure as fuck wasn't leaving it to Stepson. I reached slowly for my police radio. 'But first... Just let me get the boy some help.'

'I just want to go home.'

'I'm afraid I can't let you do that,' I said, as my fingers brushed against my receiver.

'Don't!' he warned, his hand reaching for the knife.

Beside me Stepson bristled, one leg forward, bent at the knee.

I have some medical knowledge. Not very much, but enough to know that any touch of the knife, any movement, could nick an artery or an organ, and prove fatal for the boy.

The man flexed his fingers over the knife, his eyes fixed firmly on Stepson. I took a small step forward and sideways, effectively blocking Stepson, so he had no choice but to look at me.

'I'm not calling anyone. It's just me and you,' I said. 'Please. Just be calm.'

'Give me your radio. Both of you,' he demanded.

'You're out of your mind,' Stepson shot back.

'Now!' he said, as he eyed Conrad, showing us exactly what he was capable of.

'Just do it, Stepson,' I said, unclipping and placing my police receiver on the bed.

'This is a fucking joke,' Stepson muttered under her breath before slowly doing the same.

The man's hand moved away from the knife

as he collected them. He turned off both police receivers and placed them out of our reach, on top of a chest of drawers behind him.

'Can you tell me your name?' I asked.

The man thought about my question and opened his mouth to speak, before shaking his head. 'I just want to go home.'

I exhaled. I was failing. My mind went blank. I didn't know my next move, and I knew Stepson was itching to step in.

Just as the unconscious boy looked younger, this man, who was six foot plus, with muscle to boot, looked older now. I wondered about their relationship. A middle-aged Asian man, and a white student. What dispute could be so serious as to lead to this? Did it start with words and build into something so horrifying?

'Idris,' a voice hissed behind me. I ignored it. 'Oi, Idris!' I turned my head a little to look over my shoulder.

Jay had entered the room.

'You shouldn't be here,' I said.

'I need to chat to you.'

'Not now, Jay.'

'Get the hell out of here!' Stepson screeched.

Jay took a step closer to me, and for a second I thought that Stepson was going to beat the shit out of him with the baton. The way he was nervously looking at Stepson, I think he feared the same thing. He stood behind my shoulder, and I could feel his hot breath in my ear. He quietly said, 'I think his name is Hussain, and I think I know what this is about.'

Chapter 10

Jay

Downstairs, by the sounds of it, the party was still in full flow. Nobody seemed to clock on to the fact that the host was dying, or dead. I couldn't tell.

The music moved through the house and the bass thudded as hard as my heartbeat. I closed the bedroom door gently, muffling the sound, and allowing me to gather my thoughts.

'Are you sure?' Idris asked, peering at me over his shoulder.

When I first saw the Asian man enter the house, a moment after I did, in my head I'd formed a picture. It was of a pissed-off neighbour tossing and turning in his bed, unable to get in the few hours' kip he desperately needed before he had to get up at five in the morning for his shift at Heathrow airport. No sleep, because some little shit next door had decided to throw a house party on a fucking Thursday!

I expected the man to give Conrad a bollocking. At a stretch, a slap. God knows he deserved one. But Conrad had taken punishment, and then some. His left eye was swollen shut and his head was put through a mirror, and now he had a blade poking out of his ribs.

This was more than a neighbourly dispute. This was personal.

And it came down to Sahira Hussain.

I think.

Maybe this man was her father or her crazy brother. Either way, it was hardly surprising that he would get so fucking vexed. A relationship between a white boy and an Asian girl can be enough to start a war, but throw in a baby? I swear, the impact is not worth thinking about.

I didn't expect this, though. I didn't expect it to go this far.

'Either you get rid of him, or I will,' Stepson snapped.

'Wait!' Idris said. 'Jay, are you sure?'

I was starting to feel very much like I was getting in the way. I had to get this right. My eyes were now fixed on the man. I could see every emotion in his face. Gone was that look of fury from earlier, and it had been replaced with pain and regret.

I took a small step forward until I was standing

beside Idris. The man's eyes followed my every movement.

I think it's a cultural thing, but an Asian man of a certain age is given respect by the next generation, whatever their relationship, and that respect comes in the form of one word.

Uncle.

Mr Jalali who deals pirate DVDs out of Apollo Video. *Uncle*. Mr Agrawal, the newsagent who sells duty free fags from under the counter. *Uncle*. They don't have to be low-class criminals. Those are just the examples that popped into my head, but that word results in an instant impact in building a relationship.

So that's how I started.

'Uncle,' I raised my hand, as though I was greeting a family friend from across the street. I noticed his eyes soften.

'Zaidi!' Stepson hissed. 'What the hell is he playing at?'

Idris gave me a look. He's not what you'd call your typical Asian. His views are a little skewed, not helped by the fact that he's part of the fuzz. I returned his look with one of my own, one that said *trust me*. One only a close friend could understand.

Idris shook his head, but didn't go as far as to stop me.

'I'm not a cop.' I smiled at Hussain. He didn't return it. It was too early. But he did nod, probably glad to be chatting to someone not decked out in police uniform. 'I saw you earlier, downstairs, and I thought you were just a pissed-off neighbour trying to shut the party down. And I was like, *shit*, I've got a bag full of weed I need to shift. This guy's going to fuck up my night.' I laughed nervously, and I was alone in doing so. I cleared my throat. 'But that's not why you're here. Is it?' He blinked blankly. 'You're here because of Sahira.'

He didn't take his eyes off me, even as a tear rolled slowly down his cheek. He ran a hand over his face. The man pretty much confirmed his name was Hussain, when he said, 'She's my baby.'

I get it. In his eyes Sahira was still his baby, and it was impossible for him to think that his baby was carrying a fucking baby. But it's not like that. Strip away religion, and upbringing, and the cultural differences, and you'll find that Sahira was as much to blame as that arrogant dick, Conrad. Scratch that! Considering who she was, Sahira should have known what would happen. But, as they say, love makes you do strange things. Apparently. I wouldn't know.

Obviously, I didn't share my thoughts with him. Instead I nodded that I understood.

'He looks pretty fucked up,' I said, nodding my head towards Conrad.

'I didn't do it,' Hussain said, pretty fucking convincingly, even though all arrows pointed at him.

'He still needs help,' I shrugged, non-committal at best, and my eye caught movement on the bed. A twitch of the shoulder. Just a touch. Enough for me to take a step back, as though Conrad was about to rise from the dead.

He slowly opened his one good eye. The other was still pummelled shut. His lips moved as though he was trying to say something. Instead a weak, raspy breath escaped from his mouth. Hussain moved closer, leaning over him. Stepson was about ready to explode, as Hussain placed his ear close to Conrad's mouth.

'Step away from him!' Stepson cried desperately.

Hussain shot up a stern finger, loosely meaning *shut the fuck up*. His eyebrows furrowed and his face twisted as he tried to understand the words coming out of Conrad's mouth.

Hussain nodded. And then surprised the fuck out of everyone by gently moving Conrad's blond hair out of his face. In another world, this was a man caring for his future son-in-law. Just not in this world.

Hussain straightened up to his full height.

'What did he say to you?' Stepson said, her arms stretched out, the canister pointed squarely at Hussain.

The man took a moment before answering. 'He said... Hannah.'

Chapter 11

Idris

Conrad's eyes closed, and his head dropped, as though saying that name had exhausted him. Thankfully, he was still breathing, but I didn't know how much breath Conrad had left in him.

We didn't know what that name meant until Jay said, 'I know Hannah.'

'Who is she?' I asked.

'She's his girlfriend,' Jay said. 'No, not his girlfriend, but a friend who really wants to be his girlfriend. I think. I don't know.'

The right thing to do would be to get rid of Jay, but he seemed to be in the know, which meant he was one step ahead of us. But I was starting to see the picture.

'Blonde girl?' I asked. 'Mousy features.'

'That's a bit harsh, but yeah, that's her.'

Beside me, Stepson nodded. 'She was in the room after your mate got slapped around.'

'He's not my mate,' Jay was quick to add. 'Just right time, right place.' He shrugged.

'Yeah, wonder what you were doing here in the first place,' Stepson said, unwilling to let go of the fact that Jay had been dealing.

'Bigger picture!' I said. 'Hannah could still be here.'

'I'll find her,' Jay said, spinning on his heels so quickly that he almost did a 360. I called after him but he had already opened the bedroom door and rushed out.

'Shit,' I hissed. 'She could be dangerous.'

'Dangerous,' Stepson snorted. Her eyes intensely fixed on Hussain. Now that Jay had left, she could let loose, thinking that I'd back up any action that she took, and report it in her favour. She'd be wrong. 'The only suspect is the man who said he's going to kill him, and is now standing over the weapon.'

I could have convinced myself that she was right. The scene in front of me, and all that was said and done before, was damning for Hussain. But Conrad had spoken Hannah's name for a reason. Did he want a friend to comfort him or was she a witness?

Or was he simply pointing us towards his attacker?

I couldn't put any thought into it, as Hussain

was slowly crouching down low beside the bed. 'Back away, mate,' I said. 'Just stand back against the wall.'

He ignored the order, just as he had done with every other order that was put to him, and rested on his haunches. His eyes were level with the knife.

'Please,' I pleaded. 'Give me my radio back. Let me call an ambulance.'

'He'll be fine,' Hussain said, not taking his eyes off the knife.

'You can't know that for sure.'

'Look at it.' Hussain nodded at the knife. 'It's not even halfway in. He'll be fine.' He looked up at us from above the handle of the knife. 'You're making a mistake,' he said. 'If I was going to stab this boy, I'd make sure he felt every inch of the blade.'

His words weren't spoken with any menace, but it still made me break out in a cold sweat.

Hussain straightened up, nodding to himself, thinking God knows what. I prayed that he didn't make the wrong move, giving Stepson the chance to justify her actions. But, fuck me, he was doing just that.

Hussain peered over his shoulder at the window behind him, his body moving towards it. His eyes were off us for a moment. My only thought was that he was looking for a way to escape, and it looked like Stepson thought the same. She rushed at him with her baton raised.

My arm shot out, reaching for the back of Stepson's stab vest, but she was fast and all I could grasp was thin air. She cut the distance between them, but Hussain spotted her from the corner of his eye. The back of his hand moved quicker than the baton bearing down on him. He swung hard and fast and blindly, connecting under her chin and knocking her off her feet. She landed on her back.

I was quick to release and extend the baton for the first time in my short time as a police officer. With my heart beating out of my chest, I stepped past my partner, ready to end this.

Hussain expected it.

To my horror, he wrapped his fingers around the knife and ripped it out of Conrad's flesh.

I was deafened for a moment by Conrad's short, sharp scream of pain as he squirmed on the bed. His hand rushed to the wound and the blood started to seep freely through his fingers. The shock quickly made him lose consciousness.

My knees weakened, but I stood firm. I stood still. I had to.

Because Hussain, with a straight arm, was

holding the knife two fucking inches in front of my face.

I had lost control of the action. I was so out of my fucking depth here. The hell was I doing rushing at him like that? What the hell was I thinking, becoming a cop?

My eyes focused on the blood-tipped blade. I let go of the baton and it clattered on the hardwood floor.

'It's okay,' Hussain said, his free hand reaching behind him towards the window. 'Move back.'

I did. Gladly. Stepson gingerly got to her feet and stood beside me. The baton and CS gas were still in her hands, but lowered by her side, less threatening.

Below the window was a chest of drawers. With his free hand, Hussain opened the top drawer. He picked out three T-shirts and lobbed them on the bed beside Conrad. He picked up one T-shirt and scrunched it tightly in his fist. He gently lifted Conrad's hand away from the wound and pressed down on it with the makeshift dressing.

Stepson and I exchanged glances, accepting that we'd read his movements wrongly. Hussain wasn't trying to escape. He was trying to help.

'I'm not buying it,' Stepson said through the corner of her mouth, as blood trickled slowly down her nose. 'It's the act of a guilty man.'

I didn't commit to an opinion one way or the other. The way he'd lashed out at Stepson and then held the knife on me told me he was capable.

Hussain kept the pressure on the wound, the white T-shirt quickly became blood-soaked. 'Do you know what you're doing?' I asked.

'I've been stabbed three times. I know what I'm doing.'

'He needs a hospital,' I said.

'I walk out of here first.'

'I can't let you do that.'

Hussain nodded thoughtfully and said, 'If this boy dies. It's on you. Not me.'

Chapter 12

Jay

The party was peaking. Twice as many guests. Some fashionably late. Others, by the look of them, uninvited. I could tell the uninvited by the way they were dressed – tracksuits, Adidas Gazelles, and cheap gold Argos jewellery. I recognised a few from around town. Typical Hounslow boys who couldn't spell university, let alone attend one. They had no right being there. But if you're going to throw a house party, word spreads quickly, and next thing you know, hard-hitters are drinking their way through your stash while eyeing up your girl.

I searched for Hannah, but it was difficult to see anything through the sheer mass of bodies. I remember she was wearing a green dress, so I kept my eyes peeled for a flash of green. In the kitchen, a couple of the uninvited were accosting the invited. Playful at a glance, but with a real sense of threat behind it.

One that I recognised asked a student, 'What did you vote? Leave or remain?'

'Fuck's sake, Khan,' I said, stepping between him and the anxious student. 'Leave 'em alone.'

Khan was old, or older at least. He had a decade on me, and was probably twice as old as the students that he was scaring the shit out of. On top of being old, he was old school, meaning his brain was wired a certain way.

'Just making sure these snotty bastards know which way the wind blows.' Khan grinned at me.

This whole fucking Brexit saga had everyone twisted. There was enough division in this country as it was. Exhibit-A being the shit-show upstairs. I didn't have time to get into it. I shook my head at Khan and moved past him, squeezing past bodies until I was at the patio door leading to the garden.

I pressed my face against the glass. The back garden was as busy as the house. I slid the door open and instantly the smell of skunk hit me. I walked through the crowd, as students tried to get my attention, either to tell me how good my shit was, or to ask if they could get any more. I ignored them all, my eyes fixed on the garden swing at the end of the well-kept lawn, where a sad-looking Hannah was sitting beside a stressed-out Duncan.

He was leaning forward, knees on elbows and

head in his hands. Hannah was sitting back, her head resting back against the seat, her eyes up at the stars, Conrad clearly on her mind.

I stepped up to them. Duncan was first to notice. He lifted his eyes. 'You're still here.' He smiled, as though we'd bonded in the short time we had together.

'I need to speak with Hannah.'

Even saying her name didn't knock her out of her trance.

'After you left,' Duncan said, 'things got out of hand. Sahira's dad turned up–'

'And kicked the shit out of Conrad. I know,' I filled in. 'Did you see what happened?'

'I ran out of the room,' Duncan said, without any sense of shame, as though running away was his default response. 'I was going to call the police, but saw that they were here already. I don't know what happened after that.'

Things got fucking worse is what happened.

Duncan nudged Hannah with his elbow. 'Hannah!'

She blinked and looked across at Duncan, before her eyes moved to me. She took a moment to place me.

'Conrad's asking for you,' I said.

She shook her head heavily, as if trying to shake a picture of him out of her head.

'It's not me he wants.'

The power of those words made her bottom lip quiver, and made me feel fucking sorry for her. 'I don't know about any of that, just that he asked for you,' I said, gently touching her arm. 'C'mon.'

She shrugged my hand away as if it were a live wire. Fair enough, I often have that effect on women. I backed away with my hands up. I could see her mind ticking away. She slowly got to her feet and moved past me.

I followed her, trying not to lose her in the crowd, with Duncan a step behind me at my shoulder. I turned to tell him that his presence wasn't needed.

'Trust me, mate. You're better off down here.'

Duncan stopped in his tracks. The crowd drew around him as I followed Hannah. I stepped through the patio doors and into the house, and I could feel that the life had been well and truly zapped out of the party. This should have been prime time, people peaking on whatever drink or drug they had consumed. But instead the fucking uninvited had made their presence fully felt.

In the living room, Khan had made himself at home on an armchair, legs stretched out and feet up on a footstool, cutting the dance floor in half.

Not that anyone was dancing. Khan caught my eye with a twinkle in his. This was typical Khan, rising to the occasion. And the Brexit referendum was exactly his kind of occasion where he could thrive on division.

He was sipping happily from a bottle of Bud, while in front of him a couple of his sniggering followers played tennis using one of the students as a fucking ball. Khan raised his bottle in salute to me and grinned. I mouthed *'Fuck's sake,'* knowing that it was bound to get worse. I turned away. Hannah was already halfway up the stairs.

I rushed up and caught up with her on the landing. I should at least warn her that her beloved Conrad was in a bad way.

'Hannah,' I said. Either the music was too loud for her to hear, or she was ignoring me. She moved towards the bedroom in a zombie-like state.

I slipped past her, blocking her path to the door. 'Wait here a minute!' I said. She just blinked at me with eyes that had shed too many tears.

I pushed the bedroom door open enough to pop my head around. Both Stepson and Idris turned to look at me. They both looked like shit. Stepson had a spot of dried blood under her nose, and Idris' face was as white as a ghost. I didn't ask, but it looked like they'd both had their arse handed to them on a plate. Again!

I stepped inside the room. 'I've got Hannah outside.'

Idris nodded, and turned to Stepson. 'I'm going to speak to her in the other room, see if she can shed any light. You going to be all right here for a few minutes?'

'I'll handle it,' Stepson said, her eyes burning a hole in Hussain.

'You sure?'

'Didn't I just say I'll handle it?'

I was so busy watching them, thinking that this mismatched pair should not be working together, that I didn't notice Hannah step into the room until she had slipped right past me.

Her eyes were on Conrad lying broken on the bed, as Hussain pressed a bloody cloth against the stab wound. I braced myself for an earth-shattering scream, but she surprised me by just quietly watching. She seemed to be grimly transfixed.

'She shouldn't be here,' Stepson cried. Idris reacted by standing in front of her and blocking her view.

'It's okay, Hannah,' he said, softly. 'You and I are going to have a little chat in the other room.'

Hannah tilted her head so she could see past

Idris. Her eyes back on the boy that she clearly loved. She slowly blinked and said, 'He deserved it... I hope he dies.'

Silence fell. Eerie as fuck.

As a new suspect arrived on the scene.

Idris and Stepson exchanged a bewildered look. Idris turned to Hannah and, just as he opened his mouth to speak, the bedroom door flew open. A lady was standing in the doorway. Her eyes moved steadily around the room before fixing on Hannah.

'Mum,' Hannah said, in a small voice.

In an uncaring voice, the lady replied, 'Don't you dare say another word.'

Chapter 13

Idris

I was dazzled by the turn of events. It felt like an age since she had closed the front door in our faces. So much had happened since, that it took me a moment to recall her name.

Braithwaite. Sarah Braithwaite.

The university lecturer who'd convinced us that a police presence wasn't needed. At the time it had been a simple case of noise nuisance, but it had quickly become attempted murder – with one of the suspects being her daughter.

Had Sarah Braithwaite been so desperate to get rid of us because she had an idea of what was going to happen?

My mind ticked fast as I tried to decide.

Stepson and I had witnessed first-hand Hussain launching a sickening attack on Conrad. We'd also been on the receiving end of his fury. Twice! It was clear Hussain was a violent man who had every intention of hurting Conrad. And now he was standing over Conrad with a knife in his hand. A knife that he'd threatened me with. A knife covered with his fingerprints.

On the other side, we had Hannah Braithwaite. A girl with an unhealthy obsession with Conrad. Did she find out that the boy that she pined for had wrecked her fantasy by getting another girl pregnant? We had witnesses who could place her in this room close to the time of Conrad's stabbing. While I was in the other bedroom with Stepson, desperately hoping that Hussain didn't stop breathing from the effect of the CG gas, was Hannah overcome with jealousy to such an extent that she reacted in a violent rage?

They both had motives.

As if she knew what I was thinking, Ms Braithwaite fixed me with a sharp stare, before turning away and leading Hannah out of Conrad's bedroom.

'Ms Braithwaite,' I called after her.

'I'll go,' Stepson said, but I was already out of the door. I couldn't trust Stepson to ask them the right questions. As far as she was concerned, Hussain was the only suspect. I was starting to think otherwise.

I caught up with them just as Ms Braithwaite was taking her daughter down the stairs.

'I need to speak to you both,' I said, looking down at them from the top step.

They both turned to look up at me. Their worried faces looked alike, and confirmed they were mother and daughter. Past them, I could see that downstairs the party was sliding into its own chaos. A scuffle had broken out in the hallway between a few local Asian lads, who weren't strangers to the police, and a group of white students.

I could picture this shit happening up and down the country because of this damn Brexit referendum, but right now it was a fucking nuisance! I couldn't even call for assistance, because Hussain had taken our radios away. Even if I could, there was no way of knowing how Hussain would react if more cops came charging through the door.

I took Ms Braithwaite and Hannah into the second bedroom, and before I could close the door behind me, Jay slipped into the room. I gave him a look as though he was getting in the way, but quickly remembered that without him I wouldn't have Hannah. He was proving useful. I shut the door behind him.

'It's kicking off downstairs,' Jay said, as Ms Braithwaite sat her daughter down on the single bed and then stood beside her.

'I know,' I said.

'Shall I call the cops?' he said.

'I'm not in fancy dress, Jay,' I snapped, unnecessarily. Throughout it all, a small part of me wanted to impress my friend.

'You can't be in two places at once. You need backup.'

I shook my head. 'We've finally got Hussain to calm down. Backup arriving may make him violent.' I glanced across at Hannah. 'Let me just deal with this.'

'I would like to know the meaning of this,' Ms Braithwaite snapped, in a way I imagined she would when teaching class. 'You cannot keep us here.'

'I just want to ask you both some questions.'

I looked at Hannah first. She was in a daze and I didn't think I'd be getting much out of her. So I started with her mother.

Ms Braithwaite crossed her arms tightly across her chest and gave me a look that she probably reserved for her students. Even though I was towering over her, it was she who had a threatening presence.

'When we first met,' I started, 'you said you were here to turn the music down. You want to tell me what really brought you here?'

Ms Braithwaite kept silent. Fine by me. I had more to say.

'Why don't I tell you what I think?' I said,

stealing a line out of a hundred bad cop flicks. 'You knew Hannah was obsessed with Conrad, and she wouldn't react well to the pregnancy.' I paused, looking for a reaction. When she remained stony-faced, I went on. 'Maybe you were at home, in the kitchen, and you noticed a knife was missing. Maybe you went to Hannah's bedroom and noticed that *she* was missing. You trusted your instinct. A mother's instinct.'

'Idris?'

I ignored Jay. As I kept talking, what had happened was becoming clear. I was going to solve this thing.

'Maybe you called her phone. Left her lots of voicemails, texts... If I was to check Hannah's phone, would I find panicked messages from you?'

A flicker in Ms Braithwaite's eye. Still nothing from Hannah.

'Your daughter left the house armed with a knife. The attack on Conrad was planned, and you, Ms Braithwaite, knew it was coming.'

I stopped, pleased with my closing argument. But still a nagging voice was on at me.

'*Idris!*'

Jay. Again. Hissing behind my shoulder. I kept my eyes on Ms Braithwaite for a moment longer, revelling in my victory, before turning to Jay.

'What?' I said.

'A word,' he said. 'Outside.'

'Now?'

'Yes, fucking now,' Jay said, opening the door.

I shot the Braithwaites another look, before stepping outside onto the landing.

'What is it, Jay?' I said, itching to get back to Stepson and tell her my theory.

'It doesn't make sense,' Jay said.

'You heard Hannah when she saw Conrad. She said *he deserved it*, that she *hopes he dies*. You heard that!' I said, trying to keep the frustration out of my voice. I took a breath. 'Trust me, this is a crime of passion.'

Jay didn't reply immediately, which was strange in itself. He's normally quick to shout the odds before using his brain. He took his time to measure the words.

'Look, I rolled two joints in that room earlier, and Hannah seemed fine. I mean, yeah, she was clingy, desperate even, but not I've-got-a-fucking-knife-in-my-handbag desperate.'

'What're you saying, Jay?' I said, as I started to see holes in my theory.

'I'm saying that I don't think she rocked up to this party with a blade.' Jay shrugged. 'I don't think it was... uh?'

'Premeditated,' I said, tiredly.

'Yeah, that,' Jay said. 'However…'

'Last thing I need right now, Jay, is a however.'

'Just hear me out. When you and Stepson were trying to resuscitate Hussain… Is that the right word, resuscitate? Revive?'

'Jay!'

'Sorry, yeah, when you were dealing with Hussain in the other room, I was left alone with Conrad and Hannah. He made it pretty clear that he had feelings for Sahira, and that near enough broke Hannah. You've seen the state she's in!' Jay shrugged. 'If you ask me, she had motive.'

I never thought I'd be getting advice on an inquiry from Jay! I rubbed my hands over my face, questioning once again if I was cut out to be a cop.

'Stop feeling sorry for yourself, you sap,' Jay said, reading me just as well as I can read him. 'The fuck do I know anyway? It's either Hussain or Hannah. You tell me.'

I looked at the closed bedroom door where Hannah and her mother were, and then I looked over at the bedroom door where Hussain was in effect keeping Conrad hostage. He was a big man, and I had no doubt that if he had put that knife in, he would have buried it to the hilt. It told me the knife attack had been carried out by a smaller person.

Even if Hannah didn't bring the knife with

her, would she have been angry enough to go searching for one? Downstairs? In the kitchen? Through the mass of bodies, the loud music running through her and pumping her with adrenaline? It's possible. Her mother obviously seemed to think she was capable of it. Otherwise she wouldn't have turned up there.

'Duncan,' Jay said, breaking me away from my tangled thoughts, as a new face nervously shuffled up the stairs. 'You shouldn't be here.'

Duncan, whoever he was, looked back down over his shoulder, and swallowed.

'A fight broke out,' Duncan said. 'Somebody called the police. There are cops everywhere.'

Those words almost brought me to my knees.

I was about to find out exactly what Hussain was capable of.

Chapter 14

Jay

Idris legged it back into Conrad's bedroom. I stood sentry outside Duncan's bedroom just in case Hannah tried to make a break for Mexico.

'What a fucked-up night,' I stated the obvious. Duncan nodded, but I don't think he even heard me. He seemed to be lost in thought. 'What's up?' I asked.

Duncan pointed towards Conrad's room and mumbled something. With the music pounding, I couldn't make out what he said. I leaned in closer. 'Say that again.'

'I think I left something in there.'

'What?' I said, trying to figure out what could be so important that it couldn't wait. 'The knife?' I smiled.

He laughed. I did, too. It was pretty funny. Then he said, 'No. Car keys.'

I wiped the smile off my face. 'Why would you be carrying around your keys? You live right here.'

'I kept them with me, you know, just in case someone from the party starts to wander through my stuff.'

'Oh, okay, makes sense.' I shrugged. 'It's gonna have to wait, I guess.'

That should have been the end of that topic. But instead he swallowed and said, 'It's just… I need them now.'

'Why?' I said, a little harsher than I'd meant. 'You've had a few drinks. It's not like you can drive.'

Duncan dropped his gaze.

'Duncan?' I narrowed my eyes. 'What's going on?'

'I just need those keys,' he mumbled to the floor.

'Fuck, man! What did you do?'

He flinched and took a step back, and another, without realising just how close he was to the top of the stairs. When his back foot didn't meet the floor, he wobbled and started to fall back. The fear in his eyes matched the fear in mine as his arms flapped, as though he could fucking fly. My hand shot out, meeting his chest harder than I'd expected, and for a horrifying second I thought I was going to help him tumble down the stairs. I closed my fingers, scrunching his shirt in a tight fist and pulled him hard towards me.

'You're coming with me,' I snapped.

I wasn't enjoying this. I really wished Duncan wasn't involved, but he was acting shifty enough to suggest otherwise. With his shirt still bunched in my fist, I dragged him towards Conrad's room so he could explain himself to Idris.

I pushed the door open.

The room was bathed in blue light from the police cars lined up outside of the house. Hussain was holding the knife out in front of him towards Idris and Stepson. Spittle flew out of his mouth as he screamed, 'I told you not to call the fucking police.'

Stepson looked over her shoulder and yelled at me. 'You can't be in here. Get the hell out of here.'

Idris was standing in front of his partner, his hands up in front of him acting like a fucking shield, as Hussain drew small arcs with the knife in his face.

I wanted to help my friend, but I was frozen to the spot. Above the raised voices, and above the sound of my heart thumping in my fucking chest, I heard Duncan's small voice in my ear.

'Mr Hussain,' he said. 'I'm looking for my car keys.'

'Jay!' Idris screamed, knocking me out of my frozen state. 'Get him the fuck out of here.'

I pushed Duncan back, both my hands on his chest trying to guide him out of the room, but he wouldn't go. 'Mr Hussain,' he said, his voice grew louder as he urgently tried to get his attention. 'It's attached to a heart-shaped key ring.'

Hussain froze. 'No!' A desperate whisper escaped his lips as he shook his head, over and over. He withdrew the knife from Idris' face, and dropped heavily to his hands and knees, searching desperately for the keys. He reached under the bed and when his hand emerged I glimpsed a heart-shaped key ring, before it disappeared quickly into his pocket.

Hussain slowly got to his feet.

Idris took a step back. As did Stepson. As did I.

Hussain turned and looked out of the window. Something outside caught his eye. Something that made him open his hand and allow the knife to slip from his grip. It clattered loudly onto the hardwood floor.

Hussain turned back, and lifted both his hands above his head, and said, 'I have a confession to make.'

Chapter 15

Idris

'I did it,' Hussain said, with his arms in the air. 'I stabbed the boy.'

I kicked the knife with the side of my boot. It slid and spun across the floor away from Hussain.

'Get out, Jay!' I said, trying to keep calm. 'Take Duncan with you.'

'Shout if you need me,' Jay replied, and despite everything, that made me smile inside.

I watched Hussain as the door closed behind me. Knife or no fucking knife, Hussain was a dangerous man. Stepson, armed with the baton and spray, gave me a nod, and I shuffled very cautiously towards him, waiting for an attack.

I pulled one of his arms down behind his back, and when he didn't resist, I dropped the other arm too. 'Cuff him!' I said, and Stepson quickly clicked the handcuffs around his wrists.

I spun him round and pushed him face down against the chest of drawers under the window.

I took a breath, and for the first time in my short career, I said, 'You do not have to say anything, but it may harm your defence if you do not mention when questioned something which you later rely on in court.'

I let the adrenaline wash over me as I exhaled.

Stepson picked up her police radio and switched it on.

'Search him,' Stepson said.

I didn't think Hussain was carrying any other weapons, but I wanted to know why the keys had made him desperate enough to confess his crime. From his back trouser pocket I slipped out the heart-shaped key ring, attached to a Yale house key and a Mini Cooper key fob. I stared at it, trying to make a connection.

As evidence, it didn't make much difference. We had a confession.

Stepson radioed for assistance as I held Hussain, bent over the chest of drawers. Over him, I looked out of the window. Hordes of partygoers were leaving. A few, who didn't seem to belong, were leaving in handcuffs. The house party had well and truly shut down. A police van with flashing lights was screeching its way down the road, to join the two police cars that had already arrived to deal with the ruckus downstairs. They had parked across the drive, behind a red Mini Cooper.

I could just about make out the registration number. I looked at the Mini Cooper fob in my grip. 'Stepson. I need you to carry out a vehicle registration check.'

'What is it, Zaidi?'

'I want to know who that Mini Cooper is registered to,' I said, nodding my head at the car.

Hussain shook violently under my grip. 'I've already confessed,' he cried. 'Take me in and fucking charge me!' I kept him held down until his face was pressed against the surface of the chest of drawers.

And I read out the number plate.

Stepson turned away and made the call. I looked down at Hussain and noticed that I was pressing too hard on the side of his face. I eased the pressure. He looked at me from the corner of his eyes. They were wet with tears.

'Please, I beg you, don't do this. I wanted to kill him. It was me. It was all me.'

From Stepson's radio, a cracked voice came through.

'Red Mini Cooper, Kilo Zulu One Five Foxtrot Sierra Yankee is registered to a Sahira Hussain.'

Chapter 16

Jay

On the landing, Duncan was sitting against the wall with his knees tucked under his chin. I paced the small area, trying to burn off the nervous energy. 'What the fuck?' I repeated, trying to get a grip on what had just taken place. 'What the fuck?' I couldn't believe after all the drama, Hussain had simply decided to confess that he had tried to kill Conrad. '*What the fuck?*'

'It's my fault,' Duncan said.

I had no doubt that Duncan had played a part in this. Whether it was intentional or not, I didn't know. I doubted it. I stopped pacing and stood over him, but that felt a little threatening, so I moved next to him and slid down the wall and sat beside him.

I waited.

'I called her…' he said. 'Earlier, I phoned her.'

'Who?'

'She's a mate! I couldn't not tell her what they

were saying about her, what they were planning. She had a right to know.'

I clocked on. 'Sahira?' Duncan nodded weakly. 'What did you say to her?'

Duncan bottled up. Didn't say another word. He didn't have to. I knew what it fucking meant.

I was witness to it.

I'd watched Hannah hopelessly fawning over Conrad. I heard them as they discussed abortion. Had Duncan, in his duty as a friend, told Sahira everything? It looked pretty much like he had.

It looked like Sahira had more of a motive than anybody else.

I could picture Sahira rushing out of Conrad's room, running out of the house, only to get to the car and realise that she'd left her car keys at the fucking crime scene. In a state of blind panic on her own, she'd called Duncan. And the friend that he is, he came sniffing back to fetch them.

And being the father that Hussain is, he'd confessed to his daughter's crime.

For fuck's sake! Remind me not to fall in love.

I got to my feet, pulling Duncan up to his, as boots stormed up the stairs. A mixture of cops and medics. Stepson stepped out of Conrad's room and gave them instructions.

The medics entered Conrad's room and two

uniforms went into Duncan's room, removing Ms Braithwaite and Hannah, and taking them down the stairs. Stepson took Duncan by the arm and followed.

When they were out of sight, the door to Conrad's room opened and out stepped Hussain. His hands were cuffed behind his back, as Idris guided him.

I caught his eye, and he gave me a nod as he walked past. I was proud of him – obviously I'd never say that to him, it's not the kind of relationship we have. Like most good friends, we're more comfortable ripping each other to shreds.

But it got me thinking. The paths that we had set out for ourselves led in very different directions. I had this bubbling feeling in my stomach that a time was coming when our friendship would be put to the test.

Chapter 17

Idris

In the movies when a cop makes a bust, he goes back to the office to hearty pats on the back and cheers of delight. All those doubts quickly disappear and a newfound respect emerges among their peers.

Yeah, well, that shit truly only happens in the movies.

As news of the night's events filtered through, all I received was not-so-discreet shakes of the head and hushed whispers. *Why didn't we request medical assistance and backup sooner? Why hadn't we contained Hussain when we first had him?*

Stepson and I sat at our desks and filled out our reports in silence. Stepson hadn't tried to convince me of her version of events. It wasn't because she trusted me. It was because she and I knew that my dear fucking colleagues would make my life hell if I turned against one of our own. It didn't matter that Stepson used the CS gas at will and without just cause, but still I left *excessive force* out of my report. I had to.

On the flipside, and there's always a fucking flipside, Stepson didn't mention that I wasn't keen to bring Jay in on suspicion of drug dealing.

I gave the report a once over and uploaded it.

'How's it coming along?'

I looked up to see DCI Elliot peering over my shoulder.

'Just uploading it now, Guv,' I replied, trying hard not to meet his gaze.

'Don't worry, Zaidi,' he said, with a hand on my shoulder. 'A rookie cop makes rookie mistakes.'

His words didn't make me feel better, but they didn't make me feel any worse.

I finished my shift and walked out of Hounslow nick around six a.m. A ten-minute bus ride, and I was home. Ten minutes after that, with my police uniform in a heap by my bedside, I was asleep.

I woke up almost twelve hours later to find that the people of my country had voted to leave the European Union.

*

Two short sharp bursts of the horn. I peered out of the kitchen window, and saw Jay waiting in his car. I gave him a finger, telling him to wait a minute. He returned it with a finger telling me to hurry up. I knocked back my tea, told Mum not to wait up, and stepped out of the house. I was looking forward to having a low-key night chatting breeze and shooting some pool.

As I walked to his car, I noticed over the roof a black motorbike parked about twenty metres behind Jay's Nova. Even from that distance, I could hear the low growl of the engine. I didn't recognise the rider from behind his dark-tinted visor, but I was pretty sure he wasn't a neighbour. He just seemed to be... waiting. I found it odd. Possibly it was that copper's instincts I kept hearing about. Maybe I was developing a sixth sense. Or most likely, after the previous night's events, I was being paranoid.

I got into the car.

'Whas up, Jay?' I said, as we bumped fists.

'Quick detour first,' Jay replied, as he turned the key and the Nova spluttered to life.

The detour took us through Heston to Highfields Estate. I kept an occasional eye on the wing mirror, checking to see if the biker was there. He wasn't.

Jay parked the car in a rundown car park, under a tower block, where his crappy Nova comfortably fitted in with all the other crappy cars. Jay sparked up a pre-rolled spliff and cracked open his window.

I knew Jay was there to deal. I shook my head and didn't say anything, but I was no longer comfortable being put in that position. If I wanted to make something of myself, I had to remove myself from these settings.

I let it slide, but that would be the last time.

'Where to fucking start?' Jay said, searching for his customer through the windscreen. 'Last Thursday was crazy! What happened after?'

'Stepson and me followed the ambulance carrying Conrad to West Middlesex Hospital. A couple of coffees in, and he'd been patched up and was fully conscious.'

'Did he say who–'

'He didn't say shit! His old man turned up armed with a high-flying lawyer, who advised him not to say a word.'

'Figures,' Jay shrugged. 'He's worried if he points his finger, some mad relative is going to chop it off. What's going on with Hussain? Is he still taking the hit?'

I nodded. His confession hadn't changed. I'd learned that Adnan Hussain had history. Two stints in prison in his early twenties, one for ABH and the other for GBH and concealing a weapon. It didn't matter that since the birth of his daughter in 1997, he had been clean.

I knew that we wouldn't be using police resources to inquire any further. And I knew that no matter what I said, it wouldn't make a difference. Adnan Hussain would be convicted solely on his confession. One he made to save his daughter, and to save the grandchild that she was carrying.

'Heads up,' Jay said, as a figure approached and crouched down by his window. He greeted his customer. 'What's happening, Saif?'

'Pack your bags, bro,' Saif grinned. 'It's only a matter of time before we're all kicked out of the country.'

'Don't be stupid. I'm as English as the Queen, mate,' Jay replied, almost defensively and slipped him a small bag of skunk through the window.

Saif laughed and, in return, handed Jay a crumpled twenty.

'The people have spoken,' Saif said. 'They want their country back.'

Jay nodded, and at a loss for words he simply said, 'I'll see you later, yeah?'

'I hope so.' Saif smiled, and walked away.

Jay fidgeted in his seat, as he watched his customer walk away. 'Do you think he's right?' he asked.

I snorted through my nose. 'You should know better than to listen to the likes of him.'

Jay nodded, silenced for now, but I could tell that it was bugging him. He started the car and we made our way down to the pool club in Chiswick. After a few minutes of silence, and sitting in heaving traffic, Jay turned to me and said, 'I'm not going to lie, I haven't a clue what Brexit means. Do you?'

I tried to get my head around what it meant. What the motive was behind the people who had voted to leave. And how it would affect us.

'Honestly, I've no idea,' I said. 'I'm sure it'll all become clear over the next few days.'

At that, Jay scoffed. 'You think so?'

I didn't want to talk about it any more. This was my night off and I needed to de-stress. I turned away from Jay and looked out of the window. My eye caught the wing mirror, and among the heavy traffic, I noticed the same black motorbike, a few cars behind us. It was sleek enough to be weaving in and out of traffic, but it was sitting still among the gridlock. As though it was waiting.

I looked across at Jay.

'What?' he asked.

'I think we're being tailed,' I whispered.

'What you whispering for?' Jay laughed, as he

checked out his surroundings in his rear-view. 'Where?'

'Black motorbike, about six cars back.'

'Fuck, Idris, it's a one-way road, every car's going in the same direction,' he joked. 'No one is following no one. You're being para! Just chill, yeah.'

That was what I needed to hear out loud. I was being paranoid. I took my eyes off the biker.

'You're probably right,' I said.

'You damn right, I'm right! I'm not being watched, *right now*,' Jay said, flashing me a smile.

'What's that supposed to mean?' I asked.

'A few more Gs and I'll be cruising Hounslow in my new black Beemer,' Jay said. 'That's when all eyes will be on me.'

ACKNOWLEDGEMENTS

It's been an honour and a privilege to work with The Reading Agency and Quick Reads on such an important initiative and one that is close to my heart. Thank you, Fanny Blake, for allowing me to be involved, and I hope, together, we can make a difference.

This was the first time I have written a short story and I thought it would be a nice break from writing novels. I was very wrong. It was a lot trickier than it sounds but luckily I had a great team to pull me out of the many holes I found myself falling in. Thank you, Katie Seaman, Jamie Groves and David Reynolds, for knocking this story into shape.

I wouldn't be here sharing my stories with you all if it wasn't for those that believe in me. Thank you, Lisa Milton and the HQ Team, Julian Alexander and The Soho Agency. Most importantly a huge thanks and debt to my family, especially my two boys who remain my biggest inspiration.

I'll sign off as I usually do with a nod to The One. Thank you for keeping an eye on me. On us.

Enjoyed THE MOTIVE?

Don't miss the first book in the series,
EAST OF HOUNSLOW

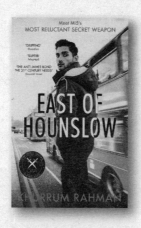

Meet Jay. Small-time dealer. Accidental jihadist. The one man who can save us all?

Javid – call him Jay – is a dope dealer living in West London. He goes to mosque on Friday, and he's just bought his pride and joy – a BMW. He lives with his mum, and life seems sweet.

But his world is about to turn upside-down. Because MI5 have been watching him, and they think he's just the man they need for a delicate mission.

One thing's for sure: now he's a long way East of Hounslow, Jay's life will never be the same again...

1

My name is Javid Qasim. I am a Muslim, a British-born Muslim.

Do you know how many times I have been pulled over by the police since 9/11? Once. And that was because I was nonchalantly jumping lanes without indicating my intentions to my fellow drivers. I got a ticking off from the fuzz, who were quite happy to forego the paperwork and give me a friendly warning. They didn't even search my car, even though the stench of skunk was unmistakeable. To this day I am proud to say that I have never had my fingerprints taken.

Do you know how many times I have been racially abused since 7/7? Not even once. I get called Paki every day, but not in the *what the fuck did you call me?* way. In my circle it's a term of endearment. You see, we know who we are. And what some may see as an insult, we see as a badge of fuckin' honour. The word Pak means pure and the word Pak means clean. And if you didn't know that, then consider yourself educated.

I'm not stupid or naïve. I am aware of exactly what is happening around me but you've got to play the game, otherwise you might as well carry a big fat *kick me* sign on your back. Don't walk around wearing a sodding shalwar and kameez with a great big dopey beard and drive around in a fuckin' Honda. That's when you get pulled over and that's when you get racially abused. But not me. Why? Cos I play the game.

I know the plight of my Brothers and I know the struggle of my Sisters and I feel for them, every fuckin' one of them. *But what do you want me to do about it?* No, man. It's not my war. Call it religion or call it politics or call it greed. It all amounts to the same thing: bloodshed, devastation and broken homes. Why would I want to get my head into something like that? Especially since my life has basically been one sweet ride – not too different from my latest acquisition, a black BMW 5 series. It's only two years old, less than thirty on the clock and it's comfortable as fuck, which is essential in my line of work, as I spend a helluva lot of time in my car. It's my mobile office. I picked it up for a cool twenty G. I paid over the odds but fuck it, I could afford it as business was ticking.

I was sitting in my ride at the back of Homebase car park in Isleworth, West London, waiting on a customer. He was late, which would normally piss me off but I was otherwise distracted by all the shiny buttons and gadgets on my new whip. The speakers sounded sik and my nigga 'Pac never sounded so good as he rapped about dying young. I clocked my patron approaching and I couldn't help but frown. This was exactly what I was talking about. He's wearing a plain white suit shirt tucked into his tracksuit bottoms, finished off with a pair of Bata flip-flops, looking like he just stepped off the fucking boat. I know for a fact that he's forever being targeted because he looks like a fucking freshy. No one likes a freshy.

He looked around the car park and I realised I hadn't told him that I'd replaced my Nova. I flashed my lights at him and his smile widened at the sight of my Beemer. He approached and walked around it, whistling appreciatively, taking special notice of my customised rims. I slid my window down and told him to get the fuck in. He did and he slammed the door, hard. I bit my tongue.

'Salaam, Brother.'

'You're late,' I said.

'Sorry, Brother, I just came straight from the Masjid. Didn't see you there. Then I remembered it's only Thursday. You only ever come for Friday prayers, Javid,' he said, laughing at the unfunny observation.

We shook hands and the deal was done. He left with a fistful of Hounslow's premium and I with a fistful of dollars. He slammed my door and toddled off in his ridiculous outfit. I hate that fuckin' sanctimonious prick. In the space of a minute he vexed me twice. Firstly, he took a swipe at me because I don't go the Masjid day in, day out. It doesn't make me any less of a Muslim than he is. So what if he decides to grow a beard and I decide to grow marijuana? I'm still a Muslim. I couldn't care less if you sit in Aladdin's eating your Halal Inferno Burger whilst I sit in Burger King eating a Whopper. I am still a Muslim. I'll drink when I want, I'll curse and I'll fuck and I'll gamble and I'll get high. So what?! Read my lips. I. Am. Still. A. Muslim. I believe in Allah and only He can judge me. Not you. Or anyone else who walks this land.

Secondly, he called me Javid. No one, but no one, calls me Javid, not even my mum. No self-respecting drug dealer is called Javid. No playa is called Javid. Girls don't wanna be giving out their phone number to a guy called Javid.

Seriously. Call me Jay.

2

I woke up in my own sweet time. I rubbed the shit out of my eyes as I ran my tongue over my pearly whites, which were anything but. It was Friday. Day of worship, day off from my daily dealing. On Friday I should be clean and my thoughts should be pure, which is not easy especially as Katrina Kaif, Bollywood sex siren, was staring down at me, wearing a sheer sari, which had obviously been soaked whilst she was out singing and dancing in the heavy downpour. Her sari clung to her every arc and her smile was greeting me with more than just a good morning. I resisted the urge, instead averting my eyes to Malcolm X, looking dapper in his black suit. The quote emblazoned at the foot of the poster read: *If you're not careful, the newspapers will have you hating the people who are being oppressed, and loving the people who are doing the oppressing.* Boom. There you have it. What a fucking line.

I don't know much about Malcolm X, but he was a Muslim and made shit happen *and* he was friends with Muhammad Ali. I mean, how many cool points is that? I had a couple of books on his life knocking around somewhere, which I hadn't got around to reading, but I have seen the movie a coupleof times. Denzel Washington's portrayal was on the button.

Prayers were at one. Sutton mosque was only a mile away but I still had to allow myself at least half an hour travel time because Friday prayers are always packed and there's always traffic as Hondas and Nissans jostle for parking spots. I stayed in bed for a touch longer and browsed through my phone, hungry customers requiring merchandise. *Sorry, not today. Hit me up tomorrow* was my token reply. There was a text message from my mum, asking me if I wanted eggs for breakfast, sunny side up? *Oh yes please* was my response. She came back with: *Well you better go to the shops and buy some eggs*. I could just picture her downstairs in the living room, chuckling to herself whilst watching Phil and Holly. My mum is pretty cool; she ain't like the other Asian parents where it's all *education, education, education*.

We've lived in the same house, just the two of us, all my life. I'd be hitting thirty in a couple of years but I had no intention of moving out. Have you seen the house prices? Fucking obscene! No shame living at home with your mum, especially if you're Asian. It's the norm. I may not be where I expected to be by this stage of my life, but, you know… Fuck it! Got my health, a few quid in my pocket. Life ain't so bad. Well-doers telling me to knock dealing on the head, find a real job, *get out of my comfort zone* – the fuck I want to do that?

My old man died in a motorbike accident whilst I was still warm and developing inside Mum, so I never actually got to see him – so it's not like I lost him because, really, I never had him. They had an arranged marriage and the accident occurred within the first year. Mum wasn't too cut up about it either, as she once told me that she *hadn't got around to loving him yet*. Anyway, Dad died. The world spun along and Mum and I spun along with it.

Mum doesn't treat me like a child, but on the flip side she doesn't treat me like a man either. To her, I'm somewhere in-between. I realise that she dates and isn't averse to a night out, and I know she knows that I'm out there getting up to all sorts, but as long as I'm not bringing the police to the door, and she's not bringing guys home for me to call *Dad*, then it's all good in the hood. We keep out of each other's business, adhering to our unsaid rules.

In preparation for prayers, I took a thorough shower, the water hot enough to cleanse away all of my bodily sins. I rubbed and I scrubbed to compensate for my colourful lifestyle. I didn't drink the night before because I did not want to be hungover at prayers, but I did party hard and I did toke hard and at the end of play, in the back of my Beemer, I spent some quality time with a half'n'half girl, christening my new car whilst listening to fuckin' Beyonce, who, by the way, I can't stand, but the chicks seem to like all that girl empowerment crap. I'm all for it. What do I care?

I brushed my whites twice in the shower and tried to get rid of the lingering taste of her in my mouth, concentrating in particular on my tongue, which felt like it was about to fall out of my mouth. My final act was to go to town down below – I have to be free from any sins. Have to be Pak.

It's only on Fridays, when the Shaitan – *Satan* – is banished from my thoughts and replaced by Farishta – *Angels* – that I seem to spend all day feeling guilty. I put on my cleanest clothes: loose dark blue jeans with a plain black T-shirt. The tee has to be plain – no depiction of any unbelievers. That's what Mr Prizada, the guy who runs the newsagents and after-school Islam Studies, used to tell me back in the day. I selected my aftershave carefully, ensuring that there was no alcohol present. I chose my rattiest, tattiest, vagabond sneakers, as they would be off and shelved as soon as I entered the mosque. Muslim or no Muslim, a thief is a thief is a thief, and I've had a pair of Nike Air Jordans Limited Edition liberated from me in the past and I ain't walking home in my socks again. Lesson learned.

I was clean. I was dressed. But not quite ready. Even though I had showered and scrubbed to within an inch of my life, I had yet to perform Wudu – *Ablution*. Running order goes like this: wash hands and arms up to my elbows, three times. Rinse out my mouth, three times. Wash my face, three times. Wet my hands and run them from my forehead to the back of my head. Clean behind and in the grooves of my ears. Finally, wash each foot, three times. All this had to be carried out with the right hand where possible. Now, between Wudu and the end of prayer, if I have to visit the toilet for a number one or, indeed, a two, the Wudu is broken and has to be carried out again. If I happen to pass gas from behind, Wudu is broken. If I fall asleep, fall unconscious, bleed or vomit, Wudu is broken.

Honestly, I find it tough, and I only do this once a week for Friday prayers. Others… Well, they do this five times a day, seven days a week.

I gave Mum a kiss and walked out of the house into the cold sunshine, my trusty rucksack tight against my back. I passed my old Vauxhall Nova and gave it a loving pat on the roof. It was my first car and it did me proud. It was going to kill me to sell it. With a press of a button the boot of my Beemer flipped open and I stashed the rucksack, rammed full of bags of skunk and bundles of cash, inside. Even though I don't deal on Fridays, I still had to have the bag nearby at all times, and that particular night I had to drop off the cash to Silas, my supplier, and pick up my cut, and he'd decide whether to send me back with the leftover gear or replenish. I started the car and the air conditioning took mere seconds to kick in. I switched from CD to radio, as I couldn't have rap music and all the profanities and sexualisation that comes with it polluting my pure mind, and I headed for Sutton mosque.

*

I saw a handful of parking spaces directly outside the mosque. I double-checked the time, just in case I had turned up an hour early, and I wondered if the clocks had gone back and I was still on yesterday's time. The mosque was normally rocking around this time, with wall to wall Pakis lining the streets. Instead, it was quiet.

With difficulty, I parallel parked in a tight spot directly outside the mosque. There were other, bigger spaces but I wanted everybody to see my ride. It took me a few attempts but I finally managed to squeeze in. As soon as I turned off the engine I realised that I couldn't leave my car here, not with weed and unscrupulously collected money in the boot, so close to the House of God.

I whispered *Bismillah* to myself as I stepped into the near-empty mosque. The first person I saw was Kevin the Convert, who was stood near the shoe rack, which, like the mosque itself, was near empty. Kevin was speaking animatedly to Mr Hamza the Cleric.

'A crime reference number,' Kevin said incredulously, waving a piece of paper in his hand. 'And what? You think that is *enough*?' Kevin scrunched up the paper and looked as though he was about to throw it to the floor in disgust, but thought better of it and handed it back to Mr Hamza.

'Brother Kevin, we must stay strong,' Mr

Hamza said in that same deadpan tone that we were accustomed to when he led Friday prayers. He flattened and neatly folded the piece of paper and put it into the side pocket of his kameez. 'This is a time to keep your head and have faith. I know, just like you know, just like everybody knows, the police will not help.'

'So why call them?'

Mr Hamza smiled, revealing a gap in his teeth that, as kids, we used to rip the piss out of. 'A crime has been committed, Brother. The police have to be called. Even though it is to give us a meaningless number, we must still adhere to the law of the land that we have chosen to reside in, otherwise we are just as wrong as the sinners around us.'

I removed my shoes and placed them on the shelf. I kept my head down and walked past them into the main prayer hall.

What I saw made me sick.

Illustrated on the far wall, just above where the Imam led prayers, was spray-painted a crude drawing of two pigs. From the mouth of one, a speech bubble read: *eat me or get the fuck out of my country*. The second drawing was another pig adorned with explosives, with the caption: *BOOM*. I averted my eyes and looked up at the heavens and at the large, beautiful chandelier that had only just been purchased and installed after a whip around. Hanging from it were ladies' undergarments. With shaky legs I walked around the prayer hall, taking in the scene. Holy literature had been removed from the large bookshelf and thrown to the floor, replaced by printed images of naked women and homosexuals harshly tacked to the bookshelf. The prayer rug had been removed – offensive graffiti had been sprawled across it, I later learned – and I found myself standing on a hard, cold floor.

What should have been a house full of Muslims standing side by side, praying in harmony and perfect synchronisation to Allah, was replaced by a dozen or so Brothers cleaning.

I glanced around the Prayer Hall. I watched one of the bearded regulars bring in a ladder and hold it under the chandelier, but as there was no wall nearby he had nowhere to lean it. He shook his head in frustration as he laid the ladder down. I looked on as another regular placed a table directly underneath the chandelier and then a chair on top of the table to give enough height. Between the two of them, one secured the chair and the other climbed onto the table and then comically and dangerously scaled up onto the chair. They removed the ladies' undergarments, holding them with just their fingertips, and then swiftly disposed of them into a black bin liner.

I looked around for a familiar face and I spotted Parvez, who lived across the road from me. Parvez is by far the most infuriating guy I know and, bizarrely, also the nicest. We had history. He would hover around me like an irritating mosquito, always popping around my house unannounced. He would go on about Fear of Allah, Judgement Day, Taqwa and Hadith, amongst other teachings. He was harmless, though, and despite my efforts I couldn't not like him.

Parvez was knelt down, picking up broken prayer beads and books, and not quite knowing what to do with them. I stooped down on the floor next to him and immediately started to help out. Parvez looked at me with glistening eyes and, just like that, I felt my own eyes spiking with tears. I blinked them away and placed my hands on his shoulders.

'They've stained our home,' he said. 'We must get the Masjid back to a state of cleanliness.'

'Parvez. What the f— What happened?' I said, watching my language. 'I… I don't understand. What happened?'

'Kafirs,' Parvez said, by way of explanation. 'Kafirs is what happened, Brother.'

'But, how? There's someone here at all times.'

Parvez shook his head and wiped away his tears. 'Everything will come to light in due course, Inshallah, and we will act accordingly.'

I nodded in agreement, even though I didn't quite know what I was agreeing to.

About Quick Reads

"Reading is such an important
building block for success"
- Jojo Moyes

Quick Reads are short books written by
best-selling authors. They are perfect for regular
readers and those who are still to discover the
pleasure of reading.

Did you enjoy this Quick Read?
Tell us what you thought by filling in
our short survey. Scan the QR code to
go directly to the survey or visit
https://bit.ly/QuickReads2021

Turn over to find your next Quick Read…

A special thank you to Jojo Moyes for her generous donation
and support of Quick Reads and to Here Design.

Quick Reads is part of The Reading Agency, a national charity
tackling life's big challenges through the proven power of reading.
www.readingagency.org.uk
@readingagency   #QuickReads

The Reading Agency Ltd. Registered number: 3904882 (England & Wales)
Registered charity number: 1085443 (England & Wales)
Registered Office: Free Word Centre, 60 Farringdon Road, London, EC1R 3GA
The Reading Agency is supported using public funding by Arts Council England.

Supported using public funding by
**ARTS COUNCIL
ENGLAND**

Find your next Quick Read: the 2021 series

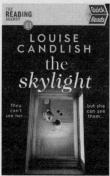

Available to buy in paperback or ebook and to borrow from your local library.

More from Quick Reads

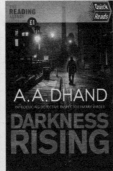

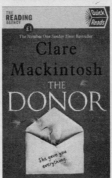

For a complete list of titles and more information on the authors and their books visit

www.readingagency.org.uk/quickreads

Continue your reading journey

The Reading Agency is here to help keep you
and your family reading:

Challenge yourself to complete six reads
by taking part in Reading Ahead
at your local library, college or workplace
readingahead.org.uk

Join Reading Groups for Everyone to find a
reading group and discover new books
readinggroups.org.uk

Celebrate reading on World Book Night
every year on 23 April
worldbooknight.org

Read with your family as part of the
Summer Reading Challenge
at your local library
summerreadingchallenge.org.uk

READING AHEAD   **READING GROUPS FOR EVERYONE**   World Book Night 23 April   **SUMMER READING CHALLENGE**

For more information, please visit our website:
readingagency.org.uk

ONE PLACE. MANY STORIES

Bold, innovative and
empowering publishing.

FOLLOW US ON:

@HQStories